THE
NEIGHBORS
WE
WANT

Also available by Tim Lane

Rules for Becoming a Legend

THE NEIGHBORS WE WANT

A NOVEL

TIM LANE

CROOKED
LANE

NEW YORK

Published in the United States by Crooked Lane Books, an imprint of The Quick Brown Fox & Company LLC.

Crooked Lane Books and its logo are trademarks of The Quick Brown Fox & Company LLC.

Library of Congress Catalog-in-Publication data available upon request.

ISBN (hardcover): 978-1-63910-473-4
ISBN (ebook): 978-1-63910-474-1

Cover design by Nebojsa Zoric

Printed in the United States.

www.crookedlanebooks.com

Crooked Lane Books
34 West 27th St., 10th Floor
New York, NY 10001

First Edition: September 2023

10 9 8 7 6 5 4 3 2 1

For Wendy Ackley and Scott Lane—
parents who always believed

PART 1
Through Windows

Something is definitely wrong

Thirsty or creepy??? The thing about Mr. Handsome is he got to be too much. It just got to the point where we never left my room. He *only* wanted to Netflix and chill. He was *obsessed* with my room. Always there. Always going to my window. We met because we both were showing up at The Turtle for 2000s hip-hop night, and he was *fun* back then. He had these glasses and this smile. But it turned into he never wants to leave my bed. It turned into "Can't we just . . . ?" Which, cool, but also, come on. I never could tell if it was because he couldn't get enough of me, or because he didn't want to be seen with me. Or was it because he didn't want to share me with anyone else? I don't know. Maybe it was all three. It was *supposed* to be just for fun. It was never going to be a long-term thing. But when I broke up with him, it was like I was some deal he was really set on not blowing up. Like he wasn't going to take no for an answer. And now he has started showing up at my house. And at all kinds of hours too. And that's just *not* OK.

POSTED BY UNKNOWN AT 3:57 PM 0 COMMENTS:

1

Adam

THE MAN SKULKING from his SUV was Kemp. It had to be. Only it also couldn't be, of course. Adam looked away and checked again, as if the view would change. And if he checked once, he had to check once more. And a third time. If the stove was on, if the door was locked, if his wallet was in his pocket. Anything with potential to be bad was worth the tic. Small fears must be petted and soothed lest they grow feral and dangerous.

Adam was up because Maddie was up. She was cranky and sleep-repellent. His Teflon baby. Furious about something. She smelled of breast milk and half-digested burps. He'd been shuffling, zombied and half-dreaming. But seeing Kemp shook him out of it. Stirred adrenaline into his slushy mix of fatigue and frustration. Red Bull into vodka.

Because Kemp was out of town. Or was supposed to be. Ali, his neighbor across the street, had told him that yesterday—or the day before? And for a week too. A business trip up north. To the land of the Amazons, as she said it, in that way that made it so obvious that it was how *he* said it. Kemp. His words from her lips. The land of Goliaths. Logicstyx HQ. Couples share everything. Even when they shouldn't.

Adam was learning that, better than most.

But Ali and Kemp weren't a couple anymore. Since when, Adam didn't know. He hadn't been exactly able to press her for details. He wasn't, strictly speaking, even supposed to be talking to her.

But he *had* talked to Ali. Like a hard, sweet candy. Gone, but he could still feel its shape in his mouth. Both in line at New Seasons, escaping the final run of artisanal chocolate and buy-one-water-a-village tumblers before checkout. She looked like she always did, only more so, the most, an abundance in jeans and a hoodie, all black, everything. Something out-of-Oregon about that. Metropolitan. Californian. Different. She was beautiful, though even just that thought felt like a bite he hadn't meant to take. It sat awkward in his throat, scratchy all the way down. There had been a moment, a brief one-two-three count, when he wondered if they might just ignore each other. He found that he couldn't; he was happy to see that she couldn't either. As she waited for the cashier to type in the codes for her bags of bulk chocolate kisses and roasted almonds, dried mangos and instant coffee mix, Ali told him she had broken up with Kemp, that he was away on a business trip. She admitted she was relieved to be free of him.

"He was getting to be a little . . . *much*." She took a breath, a small, tidy sip to feed some impulse it looked like she was fighting against. "Like, kind of . . . obsessed?"

Then her turn was over, her groceries were in her La Brea Tar Pits and Museum cloth tote, she was mating her phone to the reader, bloop-beep. The satellites all agreed: give her the snacks, she was good for them.

"You wanna donate your bag credit?" the cashier asked.

"Of course," Ali said. She wasn't a monster. Ten cents to protect the Gifford Pinchot National Forest. He knew she had been getting more design jobs; she had the cash.

"See you around," Adam managed to say.

She raised her eyebrows. *Would she? Should he?* Then she was gone.

Then it was his turn and Maddie was reaching out and tearing down packets of CBD-infused peanut butter pretzels. He'd forgotten his tote and had to buy paper bags instead, so he didn't have a bag credit to donate or not.

And yet here was Kemp, in the middle of the night. Back where he shouldn't be. Floppy hair, oversized glasses, the selvage jeans, the fitted black sweatshirt. It was a uniform he wore, no matter what, always looking like the photo heading a post on millennials and their takeover of the world. Bitcoin and TikTok. No, that wasn't right. Adam was being old. He was holding a baby. Soon it would be a walker. A medicine bottle. A handful of dirt.

Maddie fussed in his arms, a hiccupping-wail loop, a skip in the record, and he wanted to scream.

It was three o'clock in the morning on a Wednesday in November. It was starless black. She wouldn't stop howling. Seven months old and desperate for something he couldn't give her. A breast, mainly, but probably a million other things too. Being a stay-at-home dad (Adam's lame dad joke was that he preferred the acronym, SAHD with a silent H) had quickly taught him that he didn't stack up. Each day, he was judged, and each night came a wailing verdict from the lips of his daughter. Wordless rage he understood perfectly. *Not good enough! Not nearly good enough!*

He knew. Of course he already knew. SAHD Adam.

He was pacing the living room, as far from his wife, Sarah, as he could manage in their house, protecting her from the noise so that she could sleep. The breadwinner. Win me some bread. Probably, he needn't worry. The house would swallow up the noise. They had remodeled, burying themselves in debt, but it had bought them thick doors and thicker walls. A just-in-case savings account was getting smaller each month. He was scratchy-eyed and nauseous. The world was supposed to be empty, except for babies and their tortured parents.

And Kemp?

Because it *was* Kemp alright. Adam recognized his 4Runner and his slinky walk, head over feet. He went up to Ali's house, to the side of her concrete steps, and then looked right at Adam standing in his huge front window, baby in his arms. Adam froze, a nervous flutter in his throat. Usually, Kemp was almost studiously benign. Doleful eyes, easy laugh, an embodied hank of flyaway Instagram hair. Adam had long suspected it to be a mask, but still, he was shaken to see it taken off. *This* Kemp was single-minded and hungry. What long teeth he had. Something that felt like water dripped inside Adam, cold and familiar, and he held Maddie closer. She squirmed; she fought. Adam had seen this same look on his neighbor's cat once as it played with a baby crow fallen from the nest, parents cawing to insanity from above, unable or unwilling to stop their life from being destroyed. The cat was impassive to their calls, lustful and sure in his fun.

But Kemp didn't see Adam. He was invisible behind the glass. Dark night, dark house, and his neighbor Tina's motion-activated floodlight throwing glare. If Kemp *could* see anything, it was only himself.

The moment seemed to clarify into a choice Adam had no agency in making. A sensation not unlike a bad dream. Still, he was paralyzed by the feeling that he had to do something, right now, or everything would turn out badly.

Kemp *wasn't* supposed to be here.

Maddie kept howling, her tiny fists fighting the sleep sack, but Adam didn't dare rock with her lest he give himself away with movement.

And he must have been still enough, because Kemp turned, scratched the back of his head vigorously, and unzipped his pants. He peed onto the dirty, cream-colored siding. A long, high arc shimmered in the blue-white LED from Tina's house. But he didn't hold himself like he was pissing. He held himself like he was jerking off. He gripped with his whole hand, gave his dick a half dozen languid tugs, pissing through his fist. He kept his eyes on Adam's house the entire time.

A dirty troll of a feeling ran up and down Adam's spine, plucking his worries and strewing them to the ground where they wriggled for his OCD attention. *Not right, something not right, something not . . .*

Seconds—five, ten—and then it was over. Kemp jiggled himself dry, zipping up his pants. He took the front steps in twos, unlocked the door, then disappeared inside.

And still, Adam stood. Frozen. Sick to his stomach.

2

Evie

I'M SO GLAD you asked me. But, how to begin?

Well, to start, my son is a driven, special young man. Once he has his sights set on something, he'll find a way to get it. That's just who he is. Which is why it was so strange when he began dating that woman, Ali. And I don't mean to be cruel, I really don't. But Ali? A receptionist? A struggling artist? It didn't add up. Something . . . something was wrong.

I swear to you, I'm not being the typical mother, the kind who thinks her son is the most special man in the world. There goes my little prince. I am a principal of an elementary school. If there's anything the last twenty years has taught me, it's that *everyone* thinks their kids are special, and rarely any of them are.

Crispin actually was though. He was destined for great things. Did you know he was one of the first ten employees at Logicstyx? Yes, *that* Logicstyx. So to think that he would become obsessed with Ali of all people . . .

Again, I have *nothing* against Ali. In fact, what about the T-shirts? Do you know about the T-shirts? She designed this year's Chávez Elementary T-shirts. If I had *anything* against that woman, would I commission her to design our T-shirts and pay well over market rate?

They turned out fine. Thank you. But that's not the point.

It's just, I *knew* there had to be something else there. It couldn't be as simple as attraction, or, God help me, love. The other women he dated were like him. Achievers, world-changers. True stunners with bright, sure futures. The last one owned several tea shops! She was looking to expand into LA. She was amazing!

No, I suppose it doesn't matter. I'm just trying to paint a clear picture. So few actually can. I *will not* feel sorry about that. People are so eager to cancel you for telling the truth these days, and where does that get us? Everyone afraid to speak their mind, everyone scared? I refuse to back down from the truth. And the truth here is pretty simple: my son could do better.

I kept thinking, *Crispin, what's holding you to this girl? Does she have something over you? Tell me what's really going on, and I will help you.*

After all, I am, first and foremost, a mother. And a mother *always* wants what's best for her son. A mother will always do *whatever* it takes.

3

Sarah

SARAH SAT IN the pumping room, kit on her lap, and measured the weight she felt in her gut. Would she ever be free of it again? A creeping dread had slipped in like some invasive species of insect when Maddie was born. People think they are one with their body, their thoughts, their actions. A closed unit. But Sarah wasn't sure anymore. *Everything* was trying to get in. Only if she really focused, if she squared up and slammed her thinking against it, could she go on in a state of constant, sickening present tense. She put it out of her mind. She put it out of her mind. She was always trying to put it out of her mind. Or rather, to the fuzzy edge of her thinking. A good lesson to learn as a teacher. The kids didn't care what problems Sarah had at home. They needed her. The *best* her. They'd eat any other form alive. She was a master at performing. Cheerful, competent teacher in the classroom despite anything else going on in her life—fights with Adam, struggles getting pregnant, her slow, inevitable divorce from the faith her parents had militaristically tried to instill within her. Only now, she was becoming just as adept at performing outside of work too. She didn't know anymore where her real life started and the fantasies stopped.

She examined her fingers again and found dirt under her left index fingernail. She'd checked a hundred times. How in the world? She dug it out with her thumbnail, going deep enough to scrape her onychodermal band. She ran her tongue between her upper teeth and lips. Bitter pharmacy. She hadn't brushed her teeth. She really should keep a toothbrush at school. Maybe she was coming apart. Maybe she was just a new mom.

The room didn't help. Basically a closet. Dark, musty corners full of dust. It was next to the art room, which reeked of tempura, modeling clay, and cleaning products, chemical fry. Which one of these things might give her cancer one day? All of them, probably. Heat blasting, table scattered with left-behind pumping parts, the residue of other mothers' milk. An ancient poster of David Bowie, mid-leap with a book in hand, wearing a letterman jacket under the heading READ. More posters, only a little less ancient, extolling the virtues of breastfeeding. All of them slumped, barely hanging on, like the eighth graders outside, compelled to finish one last year at this school they'd known their entire lives. Why was it so humid? What were those little, black Tic-Tacs on the edges of the room? Mouse poop? Once, this had been a good idea. Support nursing mothers! Now, this room made Sarah want to switch to formula.

The single light was a bare bulb, hanging insensate from its wire, a criminal at the gallows. Sarah reached up and killed it. She couldn't pump in here. The vibes were so bad that they might haunt the milk and poison Maddie.

She would pump in her classroom. Sarah packed up her kit and emerged into the hallway. Those early-comer students, hunting hours until the first bell, watched her. Hadn't she just gone in there a few minutes before? Was she done so soon? Sarah tight-smiled and walked on, a spectacle with her little suitcase of equipment. She felt like a come-to-life poster that belonged back in the nursing room. Look! Women can do *anything*!

And she could, she found, so long as she didn't think about last night, or tomorrow. Or last year, or next. Oh she was *tired*. She felt like she was wearing ten wet cotton sweaters, alone in the snow, cold and heavy blue and always soaking up more melting weight. An inertia.

She went up the stairs and paused on the landing with the mural depicting César Chávez in a stiff, bulby style. He was their school's namesake, and he raised his arms to a field of blurry, brown workers. *Revolution! Change! By any means necessary!* Rename your boulevards, your municipal buildings, your schools. She held up her own fist, an impulse. What would this man think of it, becoming a mascot for white, upper-middle-class parents and their kids? A place where those with resources bought houses within the boundary or had mail sent to understanding friends near the school. All just so they could do what was best for their kids. Everyone was just trying to do what was best for their kids. The better the reputation, the paler a school grew; or was it the other way around?

"Sarah?"

She looked up the steps, the treads scuffed, gouged; the nosing chipped in places. There was Ashley, a fifth grade teacher, who never seemed to stop working and posted beautiful photos of them and their dogs at various bodies of water in the Oregon backlands each summer. They led the Gender and Sexuality Alliance in school and had been recently commended as a Teacher of the Year by OnPoint Community Credit Union.

"I—" Sarah lowered her fist. She just needed to finish her pumping. She noticed her outfit again. Pink pants, purple blouse. Hideous. Who had dressed her? She lived in a daze. She looked at her fingernails.

"You're early," Ashley said. They held papers. They would endeavor to make the school's finicky copy machine work. They would succeed.

"Am I?" Sarah wondered. "It's funny . . . I feel late."

Ashley laughed as they continued on, like Sarah had told a joke. But where was the punchline? She was skittering around an elementary school, looking for a place to express milk from aching breasts, dressed like a child attending a Valentine's party. And with bad breath to boot.

She unlocked her classroom door, shut it against squeaky rain boots, the hinge and crash of lockers. This would have to do. She kept the lights off, locked the door, and pumped at her kidney table. She closed her eyes, willing the release of milk to take her away, a brief, floaty nap. The machine would do everything. What even was sleep? Adam was good about going to Maddie, turning off the monitor, but the child's screams, even through their remodeled house, their supposedly overkill insulation, found her. She was always being found.

But she was too tired to sleep. Or, she worried that if she did, she would never wake up. So she read through the kids' journals from the day before instead.

Most were typical. Two sentence paragraphs about Minecraft or BTS in loopy, drunk letters, ink of every color, nib pressed so deeply into the page that the words could be read in relief. But Luke, as always, had written on for much longer, pages and pages, which was amazing, considering he'd had the same amount of time as everyone else. Sarah smiled, despite everything. Luke was an irritant, constantly pushing boundaries, asking for odd things, farting during class (he drank milk even though he was lactose intolerant). He was disliked and even feared by the rest of the staff. But he was also brilliant. And her favorite.

Sarah had a thing for the difficult ones.

She was laughing out loud when the doorknob rattled. She ignored it. Kids trying to get in before the bell. But then the scratch of a key finding the keyway, the slipping hush of pins, the plug turning. Someone with a master. Sarah fumbled her diligent, wheezing pump, disentangled herself, and spilled one bottle of milk all over Luke's pages.

"Shit, shit, shit," she said. She stood up, all of that precious work, that bit-by-bit extraction wasted. She wanted to cry. To wilt. She had told herself all her life that she was made of strong stuff. But she wasn't. This was the most basic thing she did for her baby and she'd made a mess of it. She was making a mess of *everything*.

"I didn't mean to startle you." There stood Evie Kemp, the principal, Sarah's boss. "I didn't think you were in."

Sarah looked up, and one breast popped from its shield. She tried to cover herself and contain the creeping, yellowish milk that was still, she was horrified to see, expressing, forever expressing, from her nipple. Would she ever cease to smell like milk? Unlikely.

"Here!" Evie said, gutting paper towels from the metal dispenser. "Let me help!"

Sarah wanted her boss to *leave*, but she couldn't say that. Sarah wasn't out of her probationary period yet. Every new hire had to endure two years before being made permanent. Evie Kemp could end her career. She was famous for finding ways to get rid of teachers she didn't like within a district that made firing even probationary employees notoriously difficult. She called it *making them see the light*. It was one of the reasons Chávez Elementary felt so different from the other schools Sarah had taught at. It was full of excellent people determined to do good things. Evie Kemp got rid of anyone else.

"Just, could you?" Sarah motioned to the spilled milk and stepped away from the kidney table to focus on tightening the lid on the precious remaining bottle and covering herself up—in that order. She had what the lactation consultant called a slow flow. She didn't produce enough milk. That meant she let her baby down, a little bit, every day. Which made this mess all the more painful. Fizzing worry and shame in the back of her mind. What was it they said about breastfeeding? If your child didn't get enough, they'd end up a psychopath? Or very much into cats—animal *and* musical?

Every drop was gold.

She got the lid on the remaining bottle secured, slipped in her nursing pads, and looked up to find Principal Kemp staring, paper towels bunched in her hand, having accomplished absolutely nothing.

Still, Sarah apologized. "Really sorry about that. So embarrassing."

There was a beat, a moment, a flex that implied Evie Kemp, unlike most people, was not beholden to conversational cues. She didn't need to rush and fill the gap. In fact, she probably engineered gaps as elaborate tests to judge character, mental health, and gut biome. Sarah shut her mouth. Why hadn't she brushed her teeth? Why was she so slubby? Especially compared to this tall, striking woman. Evie was dressed in an army-green jumpsuit with a leopard-print belt. It was from R13, a clothing brand they both cooed over once at an in-service, but which only one of them could afford. Evie looked like she had just stepped out of a music video.

Finally, Evie said, "Oh, don't even think about it!"

"I just—I don't like that pumping room," Sarah said. "It feels a little creepy."

"Oh, that's fine, honey," Evie said. "I *get* it. I should have knocked."

"I locked the door," Sarah pointed out.

"I know you did," Evie replied. She put down the stack of paper towels, even as the spilled milk continued its creep toward the table edge. Then she leaned over and plucked up Luke's journal, dripping milk. "Luke, huh? Kind of a little shit, right?"

"He's just too smart for his own good," Sarah said.

Evie walked to the large trash can by the door and tossed the journal in. It hit the bottom of the pail with the loud, wet slap of a wounding. Sarah looked at her, bewildered, still holding her milk.

"By the way," Evie said, looking her up and down, "I *love* your outfit."

Sarah looked down at the clash of colors. What had she been thinking? If she had just taken a little more time . . .

"And your face," Evie continued, "it's so much nicer without all that makeup."

Sarah touched her cheek. Her face. She'd been so worried about the gunk in her fingernails, her overdone princess color palette, and her bad breath that she'd forgotten about her naked face, her abandoned makeup routine. Had the bruise healed? It must have. That, or Evie was kind enough not to mention it.

"I'm going to call Dave up to clean this." Evie clicked away—three steps, four—in heels that would cost several of Sarah's paychecks. Then she turned back. "One more thing. Did Ali mention anything about Crispin coming home early? He's supposed to be in Seattle, on a business trip, but . . ."

"I don't think so," Sarah said.

"Have you seen him recently?"

"No, of course not." The worst thing that had ever happened to Sarah was Evie Kemp's son, Crispin, starting a relationship with Ali across the street. Evie had taken to coming by Sarah's classroom after school, when she was in pure panic mode, trying to get enough shit done to get out the door early enough to be considered both a good teacher and a good mother—it takes fucking *work*, kids, put *that* on a poster. Evie would slide in with questions like *Was Crispin at Ali's last night? What time did he leave? Was he scratching the back of his head?*

"It's a hard thing to break," Evie said, chuckling. "Watching out for your kids. You never really stop, no matter what. You'll see."

Then the bell was ringing, then the kids were edging in, starstruck to find the principal in their classroom, and Sarah was pulled along, into the only place she could bear. The thin, flame-edge of the present moment.

CHAPTER

4

Adam

ADAM AWOKE IN the glider chair, Maddie sleeping hot on his chest. His mouth was cotton-dry and his shirt was wet. Her diaper had leaked. Again. Sharp urine smell. Sarah had somehow managed to get ready for work and sneak out without waking them. Again. He'd thought he would catch her this time. After watching Kemp pee on Ali's house, he had been sure he wouldn't be able to fall back asleep. But when he spluttered awake and picked up his phone, the first rung of the ladder he always reached for coming back from the pool of the unconscious, she was already gone. She had texted him a picture. There he was with his daughter, both their mouths open, echoes of each other. You couldn't say Maddie was anyone's but his. Especially when she slept.

too cute, Sarah had written.

And then: i love you . . . i love you so much

can't move neck, he texted back. Power in being funny and breezy. He had so little of it these days. He felt like

he was auditioning for parts opposite a lead who was constantly changing her lines. Weeks ago, Sarah had started
sneaking out of the house for long, insomniatic walks. She
thought he didn't know. He felt it a mercy not to let on.
Where did she go? What was she looking for?

And then always these texts. These i love you's. And
what did he return with? Banter—never say what you
mean! He hated himself. What if he just told her thanks,
said I love you too? What would it cost him? In fact, what if
he went further? I'm worried about you. I feel like I don't know you
anymore. How can I help you? How can you help me? Pls help me.
Would they get back on the right track?

poor baby, Sarah texted back. He didn't need to do anything more because she got it. Of course she got it! Everything . . . everything would be OK. This too shall pass
and all that.

Adam warmed a bottle for Maddie under the hot
shush of the kitchen faucet and took her upstairs, to the
bedroom. He opened the door and felt, like he always did
recently, as if he were trespassing. A strange, airy place
belonging only to his wife. Too many pillows. White bed,
white walls, white chair. Blinding minimalism. He was
aching and thin-headed. Not enough sleep, too much
coffee. A run on the circuits. He had to poop. He put
Maddie on the bed, where she loved looking at the skylight and the dream catcher hanging from its crank. A
Native American thing that had been there when they
bought the house and had never bothered to take down,
though they would never have bought such a thing themselves. So offensive. Cultural appropriation. They would
have known better. Would they have known better? The
artifact lingered on.

What would he find if he tore it down, broke it apart, and examined all that it had netted these fitful months. What had his wife been dreaming about? Shimmering, squiggling thoughts haunting her.

Adam stepped away from Maddie and sat on their little red enameled bench by the window. From here, he could see into Ali's window across the street. He had avoided this perch lately. If not expressly forbidden, it was definitely understood by all parties to be off limits to him. But . . . whatever Kemp had been doing last night, coupled with Ali's words in New Seasons about how he was *getting to be a little much*, were good enough reasons to break the rules. He drank his coffee, cooing at Maddie, and every minute or so, watched for signs of life in Ali's room. *What did he do, did he do something, what did he do, did he do something?* The little voice inside Adam that bulleted his meandering thoughts with news breaks of all that could go wrong—intrusive thought radio—circled and sprang free every time he tried to get hold of it. Something was very wrong. Or at least, something soon would be. There were always bad things on the horizon. Always strategies he might use to avoid them by thinking the right way, by checking in, or by watching over, or, or, or.

"Aren't you a cute little smidge?" he said to Maddie. He took a big breath. His daughter was the only reliable short for his circuit of endless thoughts.

She looked at him vacantly, busy chewing a fistful of comforter.

"Good stuff?" he wondered.

She let go of the blanket and turned over, all at once, as babies do, almost as if she were falling, and made a slow-motion break for the edge of the bed.

7:45, 8:02, 8:23, and still neither Kemp nor Ali had emerged. Didn't they have work? Adam couldn't shake the feeling that the moment he left his post, something would be revealed. He needed to watch over, make sure, protect. Last night. What odd behavior, to pee on Ali's house. A dog marking his territory? Some kind of message? *You are still mine.* The way Kemp had stumbled from the SUV. *What did he do, did he do something, what did he do, did he do something, what . . .*

8:30, 9:04, 9:21, and no movement. Adam felt drifty, daydreamy, nervous. He smelled bad. He had changed his shirt but had not showered. His daughter's pee was still on his skin. Adam tapped the window. Kemp's rig, a black 4Runner with a combo code under the handle, was still parked outside. Both of Ali's roommates left for their jobs, but he saw nothing of Kemp or Ali. Perhaps, in one of the intervals when he had been getting Maddie another bottle, fetching more coffee, or checking his phone, one of them *had* slipped out. But that didn't *feel* true.

He switched to incognito mode in his browser and checked Ali's Instagram. A cascade of her screen prints. Stylized shapes and messages. Demands for justice. He liked her work. Or, God, what dad energy, thought it was "cool." Recently, her output had ticked up. She was getting jobs, garnering a following. But no posts from yesterday or today. Her most recent one, he cringed to see, like someone finding a private note in your locker and passing it around to the whole class, was *still* the print of a shadowy figure in a yellow square. He clicked his phone dark.

It was probably nothing.

"It's probably nothing!" he cooed to Maddie.

His daughter was restless. The ham of her fist, the twists of bedspread, all the toys he'd strewn on the bed, even the prized Sophie Giraffe had lost their appeal. She was counting down to tantrum. Neglected too long. She was more mobile than she had ever been and more trouble too. Constantly, it seemed, almost killing herself.

Adam took her up in his arms.

"Where has the morning gone?" he asked her. "Where has it gone? Did you take it? I bet you took it, didn't you!"

Maddie giggled. What light. Everything was worth this. The apple of his eye? An orchard of apples. Every apple in the world.

"But where did you put it? Where did you put all that time?" He lifted her above his head so she almost touched the ceiling, brought her diapered booty down on his nose, and inhaled. "Aha! That's where it went!"

And just like that, he felt a minor chord in his chest. He was a good parent, but he didn't like the actual work of good parenting. He'd ignored her all morning. His secret wish? To ignore her hours longer.

He had to put Kemp and Ali out of his mind. It *wasn't* his business. He would busy his hands to quiet his mind. It was time to make lunch. Who made lunch at ten o'clock in the morning? *He* made lunch at ten o'clock in the morning. But what was there to make? He had made everything a thousand times. What even was lunch? Mostly macaroni and cheese, sliced cucumbers, maybe some broccoli. Sliced apple and peanut butter. Milk from his wife's breasts. Not too long ago, he had been negotiating advertising contracts worth tens of thousands of dollars. Now, the prospect of opening the fridge terrified him. He went for a bag of Lay's instead and saw by a little badge on the back that it was the official potato chip of the NBA. Good for them. Maybe he should arrange official licensing for the SAHDs of the world. Slumpy sweats! Eating over the sink! Growing a little, maybe not-so-little, gut? Feeling insecure about your masculine duty to bring home the bacon? Well, *that's* the official feeling of Stay-at-Home Dads, and Lay's are the official chip!

Adam laughed to himself. Then he remembered reading somewhere that laughing to yourself is a sign of insanity. He stopped.

Maddie waved her hands in the air and screeched at him like an electrocuted seagull. She wanted the goddamn chips.

"Not for you!" he told her. "They might ruin your life."

She shrieked again.

"Fine," he said, taking down the bag. "But I warned you."

As Maddie sat in her high chair, happily destroying a small mountain of potato chips, he packed the diaper bag. The flavorless puffs, the diapers and wipes, the pad, the change of clothes, the tiny leather-soled walking shoes that were supposed to go easier on baby feet even though she was months away from walking. The bottle, the milk, the crinkly, chewable book, and the rattle. The first aid kit, *God forbid*, and knitted pumpkin hat and a pouch of pumpkin paste (you little pumpkin!) and grapes, cut in half, no choking allowed. The good camera, an issue of the *New Yorker*—one could hope—and his thermos. More coffee, too much, he was vibrating. Would have to shit soon. Burp rags, diaper cream, the little rubber Sophie that every baby had, its face mostly smeared off by Maddie's gummy bite.

But Kemp. *What did he do, did he do something, what did he do, did he do something, what . . .* The man's eyes. He'd always struck Adam as someone who held on too tightly to the things he wanted. Was he doing that now with Ali? Was he not taking no for an answer? Adam shivered, out through to his hands, mediuming an irrational terror, a premonition, a vision. He pictured Kemp in a rented van, gunning to the eastern side of the state, taking Ali out to some remote campground to do God knew what.

"OK, and we're off," Adam told Maddie. "Off to see the duckies."

They would lunch on snacks. Annie's Cheddar Bunnies would sustain them.

And yet. He stopped on the porch. Checked that he had locked the door. And again. Once more. Transitions were the worst. Always. Even when he was reading a book, he couldn't stop on a page numbered six. Get too many of those and it's the devil's number. A curse upon his house. It was in his hands. Between his shoulders. And he hated these fixations. And he held them lovingly. They demanded action, sometimes repetitive, always irrational. But the relief is in the work, no matter how useless.

He looked around to see if anyone was noticing, his hand trying the stiff knob over and over, and settled his gaze on Ali's house. It was a degrading structure on its way to being flipped one day, razed completely, replaced by a new, modern home. Thin walls, ancient electrical, slumping foundation, and a rodent infestation. The structure seemed to be staring back at him. *Do something*, it said. Ali could be in trouble. *Did he do something, what did he do, did he do something, what . . .*

Adam took out his phone and looked up the number for where Ali worked. An investment firm among investment firms in the Big Pink building. A vertical garden of money. He pressed the call button, eyeing Kemp's 4Runner the entire time.

"Smith and James and Associates, Candice speaking, how may I direct your call?"

"I'd like to speak to Ali, please," Adam said. He'd never called Ali's work before, but he had seen her behind the big desk once, laughing with Candice. He had been across the lobby and had allowed himself a glance, just one. At the time, Maddie was squirming in the BabyBjörn carrier on his chest, still more blob than baby. What was he doing there? He didn't belong. They were all making money while he was, what? Changing diapers? He went to the elevators and slipped in behind people in dark suits, rising to some random floor, singing nonsense into Maddie's warm ear, biding his time before he could turn around, slip out, and escape. He hadn't even known why he'd gone there, only that it was what he *needed* in the moment. To see her. To confirm that she was real.

"I'm sorry, Ali hasn't come in yet," Candice said dully.

"Oh," Adam said. "I—"

"Is this Kemp again?" Her words reddened, hot and breathy. "I *told* you, Ali doesn't want to talk to you. You need to leave her alone. You need to stop this—"

"No," he said. "This isn't Kemp. It's her neighbor. I was just checking."

"Adam?" she said.

And he hung up.

5

Sarah

ON HER BREAK, back in the pumping room, the little machine wheezing diligently like an iron lung to pull milk from her, Sarah tilted her head back and closed her eyes. She was washed by a relief not unlike a small high as her hardened breasts lifted from the pressure of their work, their constant, never-ending work. Behind her eyes, she traced the aurora borealis that appeared. Her thoughts buzzed, landing and tracing her worry. She could fall asleep. She called Adam instead. Suddenly, she had to hear his voice. He answered on the first ring, which was odd. Modern life. They, like everyone else she knew, communicated mainly by text.

"Are you OK?" she asked. Adam sounded breathless. "Are you running?" She felt warm from the image. A little turned on. The fit dad running the BOB around the beautiful city park.

"Running?" Adam said. He sounded confused. "No."

Of course Adam wasn't running. He wasn't interested in working out. Hadn't been since they were much younger and he was very much into rock climbing. Back when, in fact, he hadn't *needed* to exercise at all. Idling at sexy. A beautiful problem for her to figure out.

"Yes, I'm just . . ." There was a jumble in the background. A passing siren. "Maddie's not going down for a nap. We had fun . . . at the duck pond . . ."

"With the other mothers?" Sarah wondered. Adam had recently, quite by accident, fallen backward into a standing playdate with a group of moms from the surrounding neighborhoods. She imagined him being adored by these women and him being charming in response, like he was back in college. She liked this idea.

"Yeah, and—" There was a howl. A clatter of something. "Maddie. She's being so difficult. It's like she's possessed."

Ever since Adam had been staying home with Maddie, he sounded like he was lying. Even though, as far as she knew, he wasn't. Sarah didn't think he had it in him to ever lie to her again. And yet, here it was. How he sounded exactly: someone caught out.

Was he lying about going to the duck pond and seeing the other mothers? About the entire concept of marriage and parenting being fulfilling life activities? That, actually, getting fired *hadn't* been the best thing to ever happen to him? Was he exaggerating about Maddie being difficult? Sometimes it felt like they were stuck in a game of chicken, neither wanting to admit they'd had a decent day, for fear it would prove to the other what a shit end of the stick they'd grabbed when it came to dividing who worked for love or money.

"Oh no," Sarah said. "That sounds really hard."

"Yeah," Adam said. "Like, I think there's a devil inside her. I keep imagining green vomit. Head swishing around three-sixty."

Oh God. Adam *thought* he was being funny. Adam was the worst when he thought he was being funny. But he'd gotten by too long by being a little bit funny to stop now. And, of course, once upon a time she had thought he was funny too. Now he was saying that her baby girl had the devil inside her.

"I'm just really tired," Adam said, reading her silence.

"Me too, Adam."

"That wasn't funny. She isn't possessed. We don't need to call a priest. It was just a bear last night. And sleeping on the glider; it's not ideal."

"No, I wouldn't think so."

"I can't wait for you to come home," he said.

"Me too," she said. This was the closest he'd come to saying that he loved her in weeks. "Me too."

She looked at her fingernails. There was *still* something under one of them. She wanted to tell him about Kemp. But of course she couldn't.

The principal was so strange, so interested in her, that Evie had become a constant and tired topic at home. At one point last year, Adam had begged her, looking up at their ceiling as though talking to God in heaven: *Please, no more about this woman!* Boundaries were established. Rules created. If she had to vent, it had to be to someone other than Adam. A friend or coworker. Still . . . they were married. They were supposed to share everything. Even the ugly stuff. Better or worse, wasn't it written into the bylaws? Otherwise, what were they doing here?

Besides, he could always say no. He was a big boy. Or he was supposed to be.

"Listen, do you have the bandwidth for me to rant a little about Evie?"

Adam let out a breath. "OK," he said, cautiously, almost singing the word for how long he stretched it. His tone said, *I'm doing this even if I don't want to be doing this. I'm making a sacrifice, and I want you to see that I am making a sacrifice.*

Marriage is a scoreboard.

"She came into my room this morning," Sarah said. "And it was, well, it was just . . . off."

"OK," Adam said. "But isn't she kind of always a little off?"

"No, but, like, especially strange? And she saw my breast. I was pumping, and she saw my breast."

"Oh, damn."

Last year, in one of Sarah's first weeks working for the school, when she had been struggling with a troublesome quartet of frenemies in her class and putting in longer and later hours, coming home with little to give Adam, Evie had sent her a text with a picture of a slinky dress on a hanger, the edge of her naked body, an elbow and the outer limits of a hip caught in her mirror. Maybe you need a girls night out.

Then, a few weeks later, another text from her: a photo of her bare feet on pebbly ground, panties in a muddle. Skinny dipping 🐿️🦆

Perhaps the texts didn't mean anything. Perhaps the glint of bare skin, the silky pink fabric, the odd emoji combination had been a slip. But Sarah had never known Evie Kemp to slip in *anything*. Especially her appearance. She came across, always, exactly as intended.

Sarah never responded to either text and showed the messages to Adam. The joke since was that the principal had the hots for her. Which would have been funnier if

Evie didn't toggle between slathering her in good cheer
and freezing her out with deadly cold detachment *exactly*
like some jealous lover. Sarah often had the urge to scream,
*Just make up your fucking mind! Make me see the light or
count me on your side. I don't care anymore!*

And, if this morning's visit was any sign, it was getting
worse.

"Shit," Adam said. "That's . . . That's not OK. Can
you imagine if she had been a guy and he stared at your tit
like that?"

"Yeah, true, I guess," Sarah said. Tit? Come on. Of
course Adam was missing the point. He was a male, a collection of parts. He looked upon the world as through a
ViewMaster. Just change out the slide, and voila! Fresh
perspective. Clear, concise, objective answers. Everyone
could have one! It was great! Simple schoolyard logic that
had dazzled her when they first met, him a senior, her a
junior, but now just seemed . . . lazy. Yeah, so what? If . . .
if . . . if . . . But the principal *wasn't* a man, was she? So
what did that matter at all? It took the experience out of
Sarah's control and into Adam's. Suddenly it was about
double standards and about him. Could there be, oh Sarah
didn't know, huge, coordinated societal pressure against
women that made tit (ha!)-for-tat thinking inane?

"Are you mad at me?" Adam wondered. "Did I say
something wrong?"

"No!" she said. But the fireworks were in her voice. It
was, after all, encouraging that he had felt strongly about
the encounter at all. "I'm just busy. I'm just . . . It was a
strange way to start the day, and now my shirt smells like
milk. I lost two ounces."

"Maddie will survive."

"Of course Maddie will survive!"

Sarah pulled the phone away, gripped it hard in her hand, stared at the ticking clock, measuring their call. Was it enough? Would they ever count for enough? She wished she were strong enough to crumple the device up. And, actually, maybe she could. Because what the fuck? Was survival or the lack of it actually on the table? Sometimes she didn't know why Adam even bothered to talk. Shake him up and any combination of words might come out.

Instead, she brought the phone back and managed to say, "I love you."

"I love you too," he said, after a hitch.

She hung up her phone but kept it in hand. She tapped its corner against her teeth and watched the pool of weak light cast big shadows away from her pump. She breathed in, and it felt like her lungs could handle more air than before, every alveoli indulging.

She surprised herself by thinking, *I miss him. I miss us.*

6

Evie

N<small>O, NO</small>—<small>YOU DON'T</small> have to show me that stuff. I've seen it. I *knew* you'd bring up something like this. Only, it's bullshit, to be honest with you. It's people who are jealous. My son wasn't some kind of loner. If people are actually saying those things, then you're talking to the wrong people. You're not talking to people who knew him. Who rooted for him. You can make *anyone* seem like *anything* if you talk to the wrong people, or read the wrong things, or take something out of context, don't you think? We get it all the time on the playground. Kids running up, whining that so-and-so hit them. Then you hear from so-and-so and it's a completely different thing, isn't it?

Every kid on the playground has a different way they've been hurt.

Crispin was voted Most Likely to Succeed in high school. Go look at the yearbook. You don't get voted Most Likely to Succeed if you're some kind of outcast or don't have any friends. That's not how it works.

People are simple. People are so fucking simple, if you'll forgive my language. They vote in those things based on one criteria and one criteria only: who do they most wish they were. And maybe it seems silly, or juvenile, but it's not. That's how most of us spend *all* our lives. Voting for who we most want to be. Only we do it in likes, or what we buy, or how we dress. What we listen to. What we watch. Who we talk to. Who we ignore.

And Crispin won. He won in a landslide. He's been winning his whole life. That's who he is. I'm not bragging, forgive me, but I'm not. It's like I've been saying. It's about seeing the whole picture. Just look at his social media accounts. His Twitter is *verified*. Plenty of friends, all through high school and college. Plenty of girlfriends and admirers too.

I'm only telling you this because the things you're asking about, what you're implying . . . He wasn't a violent person. He wasn't alone.

Did I worry about him? No, not really. That's the thing about having a son like Crispin. He doesn't need any help getting what he wants.

OK, fine, I don't know why he wanted Ali . . . but he got her, didn't he?

His social life may have dropped off, but that's only because he was *so* invested in his job. It's completely normal in start-up culture. It's *expected* in fact. Especially at Logicstyx. The stories of that place are infamous. Bottom twenty percent cut every year. But Amazon is in talks to acquire the company, have you heard that? And, if that doesn't pan out, all of the best angel investors are lined up to go another round. He has *tens of thousands* of shares in that place. Do you know what that means? Think about it.

Sometimes, you *have* to put in the ugly work to get the big payday. It was going to change his life. He *knew* that. He wasn't depressed, he was *obsessed*. With his job. Which, last time I checked, was a *good* thing. Do you think Steve Jobs had a lot of friends when he was in the thick of it? Would you rather have your iPhone or young Stevie enjoying a more active social life?

But now you hear people talking and it's like my son was some kind of trench-coat-wearing freak who couldn't take no for an answer. That's just not right. That's just not Crispin.

No. What you're talking about, I'm sorry, is a different thing.

Ever since Crispin was a boy, he was so dedicated. I remember how he practiced Harry Potter spells in the backyard. I would watch him for hours—*hours!* He was so completely absorbed. To his little mind, the world wasn't at fault for not containing magic, *he* was at fault for not being good enough to access it. And so the only thing left for him to do was get better. Every day. All day long. To be honest with you, it scared me as a young mother. You saw other kids his age flitting from one thing to another like butterflies in a meadow. And here was my boy, repeating nonsense words and flicking a stick around.

But I know now—*that's* exactly what makes him special. The world would be a better place if more people were like Crispin. It's a big reason he's such a good coder. He's incredible. Because impossibility is not a roadblock to him. It's an *opportunity*. I bring him up in a lot of my pep talks to students. They feel so inspired by him.

I will admit that sometimes Crispin takes this same approach to people. Before Ali, he dated this woman who was beautiful and smart and successful. The tea shop owner. She's quite remarkable. And he loved her, and I loved her too. But, and I know this isn't good, she was married and had a small child at home.

I didn't know this at the time, of course not, and neither did Crispin. She kept it from him, or I'm certain he wouldn't have gotten involved in the first place. So when it came out that this woman, the tea shop owner, had deceived him, I told him to forget about her, but he didn't like that. He *couldn't* just forget her, which of course was true. That wouldn't be my son, would it? Instead, he applied himself to changing the world. Like he was still that little boy in the backyard, perfecting a levitating spell, trying to get the flick in his wrist just right, or the pronunciation of a nonsense word. To his mind, if he worked hard enough, he could change the order of reality and convince her to leave her husband for him.

He wrote her love letters, he sent her gifts, he bought a house! That's how special my son was. He wanted her to be able to step away from what she had into something even better. *Any* woman would be lucky to have him. He bought a house. A beautiful house, new construction, a few blocks off Hawthorne. Like I said, he will do *anything* it takes.

What's a stronger showing of love than that?

CHAPTER

7

Kemp

CRISPIN KNEW SHE was married from the very start of course. That fact was a problem, and he always noticed problems first. Most of his life was noticing problems before other people did. That was what made him special as a software engineer. He would sit in meetings, listening to briefs, feeling the attention of everyone at the table spotlighting him even when he hadn't said a thing yet. The project managers implicitly waited for him to give the go-ahead, clenching their teeth, fearing he might instead tear down what they wanted to do in a point-by-point logistical masterclass. There was nothing he loved more.

Sure, he briefly wondered if he might be wrong about her status—no wedding band—but that was only because she had stopped wearing her ring ever since she'd lost it on her honeymoon in Costa Rica. Much later, she confided in him that as she swam in the ocean, she watched it glitter down, down, down to the sandy bottom just like her union soon would. Platinum and diamond slicing and glancing wobbly light. She told him how she had picked out the ring on her own from Gem Set Love. Art deco navette. The one her husband had picked—Shane Co., off the shelf—was as plain as a slice of white bread. All wrong. So she had chosen one herself; made it right. Only fate had intervened with a sign. She had truly loved that ring and yet watched it go, accepting it peacefully in the moment. A brief glimpse behind the curtain: she saw the secret. She and this husband of hers wouldn't last. An easy thing to know in one instant, forget in another. But life was like that, she said. Flirting with meaning while in a committed relationship with monotony.

Crispin loved that. How she said it as well as the wedge the ring revealed. Who was this idiot who didn't know his wife well enough to pick out the right wedding band? This woman who was so pragmatic, wise, funny, and God, wasn't she sexy too?

She told Crispin she wished she had taken that sign more seriously *before* she'd gotten pregnant. With a baby, everything was more complicated.

So he *had* plausible deniability—look, no ring!—but Crispin knew all along. He'd seen her husband at the party where they met. Drunk, cornering some guy about Game of Thrones, talking *at* him about how the characters in it could be 80 years old and still kick ass. Hypothesizing that with modern medicine advancing as quickly as it was, *he* might live until he was 150. This enraged Crispin. That this man might have this wife for more than a century. The husband didn't deserve her. Worked in some kind of marketing field, but who didn't these days? Everyone a different shade of please-buy-this green. A little gone-to-seed, thinning hair, the pampered beginnings of a belly. The man's glass tilted, amber liquid tiptoeing to the edge, and Crispin fought the urge to rush over and demand that he pull it together. Didn't he realize what he was risking? Love and white carpets.

First seeing her was like seeing the sun let loose by storm clouds. Like the first long breath after a hard run. Like excellent weed in a warm bath.

She looked bored. She couldn't wait to leave. Her life was boring. But her boss was at the party, and she wanted to impress.

Well, she was dressed for it. Careful, all ye roaming hearts. A black number with geometric cutaways around her cleavage. He imagined putting a finger through a triangle, pulling down until the gauzy fabric ripped. Miraculous breasts. He wanted to destroy that dress, sex that bordered on violent. It was hot in the room. The last Friday in May and already so warm. Global warming, climate crisis, should they be scared? They should be terrified. All the windows open so guests could flit out to the balcony, feast on the view. Her skin was dewy and ripe. The salt. To lick that salt away. Crispin swallowed.

He watched her. Every moment he could get away with, he watched her.

8

Adam

ALL AFTERNOON, ADAM watched for Ali. That phone call with Candice. Undeniably chilling. Apparently, he wasn't the only one suspicious of Kemp. But how had Candice known his name? If she knew his name, if she guessed it could be him calling at all, that meant Ali talked about him. Talked about him a lot. Or at least enough. The exact opposite of what she'd told him. Which was that he rarely crossed her mind. Some poor, pathetic guppy man. That, in fact, she'd never told *anyone* about what they'd done. It was *that* unimportant to her.

Well, obviously, if Candice knew who he was, then it wasn't true. Ali *did* think about him. Ali *did* talk about him. This felt flattering and too much at once. She *talked* about him. And now she had disappeared. Maybe he was just bored. Typical housewife, fantasizing about things in the shadows, in the windows across the street. There were whole channels for this kind of show. But . . . and . . . still . . . it *felt* true. Ali might be in trouble.

He wondered what his two best friends from college, Liam and Jamie, would say about his life. This new obsession. How the mighty have fallen? Only, he'd never been so mighty, had he? But at least there had been business meetings, trips off-site to photograph impressive window installations, an implied importance to his actions. His thinking was *valued*. Literally gathered. *I'm gonna need your thoughts on this. Let's circle back with Adam. Have you run this by Adam?*

These days, it was the opposite. He was slubby, he smelled of spit-up, of urine. He never had any time. He was constantly bored.

Nobody cared about him. At home with his baby, his life was taken over by tasks that only needed his body: rocking a baby, changing a baby, picking up after a baby. They were circular, forever replenishing, renewing, never done. And right then, one to always hit her cues, Maddie cried from her crib where she had been napping. Adam sucked in air, a last breath of freedom. He went to her.

"What's woken you up?" He lifted her high, Rafiki with Simba, sniffed her diaper, the fourth or fifth time already that day. Just look at him, the connoisseur of crap. "So if it's not that, then what is it? Want a little ride?"

He strapped her into the robotic chair, the mamaRoo. Over $200! Bluetooth enabled! Five unique motions! Five speeds! Built-in sound! He fired it up. God, their credit card statement. Their poor, beleaguered credit score. When they had to have something, they *had* to have something! The machine shivered with mechanical delight and Maddie looked at him with narrowed eyes, wondering if it was the best he could do. It was. *This is the best I can do!* And he left her to it.

His work, taking care of Maddie, was better suited for a machine. Why didn't they make a mamaRoo for everything else too? They had automated devices for vacuuming, dishwashing, laundry. The dadaRoo! A cheerful robot to change diapers, put babies down, tidy up, and never ask for sex.

Ask for sex. Ask, ask, ask. As if she got nothing from it. Did she get nothing from it?

His phone buzzed. Incoming text from Sarah!

I just really love you. I just really love our life together

He "hearted" the text and started in on folding laundry, Ali's house in sight through the huge front windows, Maddie being jostled around by a robot arm. She was not happy. She needed more. Sarah wouldn't be home for hours. A Sahara away. Impossible, he'd die. *What did he do, did he do something . . .*

His hands were busy, but his mind never had enough. So it roamed. It obsessed. Was the stove on? How did he feel about the door? *Did I lock it, did I lock it, did . . .* The car's tire pressure, the chemicals in the walls, lead in the water, the stove, the stove, the stove. Was Maddie breathing? Heart beating? The fucking fontanelle. That one tiny soft spot held so much real estate in his thinking.

And where was Ali? And why was Kemp's truck still outside? *What did he do, did he do something, what did he do . . .* But perhaps they were playing hooky. Tangled in Ali's blue sheets, watching shows on her laptop, stopping to have sex or drink water. How naughty they were being! God, it was gross. Or, God, was he jealous?

Adam would have *seen* something. Kemp's little performance last night. That wasn't normal. And Ali had seemed so spooked when he ran into her at New Seasons. Or was he projecting? He felt very dead and also a little alarmed. The resting state of the Internet age.

Adam set aside the onesies, the little dresses and shirts and pants, better to just ball them up, that tiny work. He went back to the window. Sarah would be home soon enough. And when she did return, his opportunity to check on Ali would be gone. At least until the next day, when Sarah left again, and that might be too late.

Because in their house, there was no quarter for concern for Ali. And it was all his fault.

In the weeks after Sarah gave birth to Maddie, when he was still working at Lostine's Window, writing white papers on how upgrading your glass might improve your mental health, lower your heating bill, increase your home value, and other equally bullshit marketing fluff, his wife had little time for him. A stark contrast to the years previous, when she seemed to not be able to get enough. "Partners in crime" was her favorite saying. "Here's my partner in crime."

And not just the sex either. They would sit up, playing an endless game of gin rummy, keeping their ongoing score on the inside flap of the deck of cards they'd picked up in Costa Rica. *Imperial: la cerveza de Costa Rica.*

He still marked the moment, landing in PDX, going through customs, when the agent called them forward, together as a family, as one of the most meaningful of his life.

"Are you OK?" she'd asked him as they rode the MAX back to their first shared apartment, an overpriced Victorian huddle in Nob Hill.

"Of course," he'd said, hugging her close, their blocky luggage clenched between their knees lest some thief grab it and run off with their souvenir engraved coconuts and bright tank tops, both of them tanned, relaxed, sand from an ocean half a world away caught in the whorls of their ears. "It's just I realized something, in customs."

"Oh yeah?" Sarah tipped her head back. He could tell that she was waiting for him to make a joke. He was always making jokes. And this was when she still loved him so much that she would volley the joke back. Make a game of it. Or at least laugh along.

Instead, he said, "I just realized that being married means I don't have to say goodbye. I mean, not unless I want to. Like, we're one unit. Even through customs."

"Ah," she said, thrown, it seemed, by his earnestness, tears gathering in the corners of his eyes. "You. I love you."

These days, that feeling was long gone. Ever since Maddie had shown up. Adam would come home from work, sweaty and elated from his bike ride, eager to see what leaps his daughter had made in the day he had missed, only to find a disinterested Sarah, a low Sarah, a woman so entangled in her blue mood as to be unrecognizable. She didn't want to talk, she didn't want to eat, she, fuck off already, didn't want to have sex. Gin rummy? No. Movie? No. She handed off the baby, who didn't want Adam anyway, only Sarah, and retreated into the downstairs room, the TV room, now Maddie's nursery, to sit in the dark, to scroll her phone. A fisherman in black waters, hoping to land something that would feed her.

Later, Adam would troll the wake of Sarah's online activity and find a completely different person than the one sleeping—or more often not—in the bed beside him.

On Instagram, she posted beautiful shots of Maddie with captions like, obsessed with this one! On Facebook, she wrote chipper birthday updates on friends' walls. Get it, girl! On Twitter, she retweeted the latest police outrage and insisted to her 108 followers that Black Lives Matter.

During this time, she asked Adam if he had ever stood at a street corner and thought about stepping in front of a bus. Adam said of course not, and then told her that she should consider journaling. For her feelings. It was the wrong thing to say.

"I need fucking drugs, Adam. I'm depressed."

"I don't know," he said, like it was his choice. Like he knew anything about it. But growing up in his family, feelings were hurdles, and if they were tangling you up, you just weren't jumping high enough. He'd never once seen either of his parents cry. Meanwhile, he could raise koi in a tank filled exclusively with Sarah's tears.

"It will help me," Sarah said.

"I just don't like the idea of maybe the drugs getting into the milk, or into Maddie." But that wasn't it, was it? That was just an unimpeachable concern on which he could stand. To rely on drugs meant he wasn't enough. That their life wasn't enough. Also, wasn't it weak? If you couldn't control your feelings, what did that say about your ability to control anything else?

"I want to be better," she said.

"OK," he told her. "Do it, whatever."

When he told Kelly about this, the sales guy at work with an eye-popping five kids at home, he laughed and told Adam that Sarah had done the hard work for nine months. Now it was his turn. Let her take whatever. Buy her fucking heroin if that was what she wanted! Ha-ha.

"I wish I could say it gets easier with the next one," Kelly continued. "I wish I could say that, man."

So Sarah started on Zoloft and Adam did the hard work. Or tried to. After he got home, already mind-numb and agitated from a full day trying to get neanderthal construction goons to choose Lostine Windows over a plethora of others that looked, or rather looked through, exactly the same but went for half the cost, he put in an extra shift. Sarah sat in her dark room, mute and silent, ignoring Maddie's cries, Adam's fumbling attempts to soothe her. He strapped his daughter to his chest and cleaned the house, made dinner, put Maddie to bed. Was any of it helping? He didn't think so.

And then, house quiet, Maddie finally asleep in the crib at the foot of their bed, his wife still hours away from chastely joining him, Adam sat on the red bench from ancient China and stared out at the street. People coming and going. The bike riders, the runners, Mr. and Mrs. Leon trundling down the sidewalk on their post-dinner walk, Mrs. Jenkins pruning her roses, Tina squealing up to her house in one of her ever-rotating carousel of cars. Everyone firmly in possession of a life. This leafy, picturesque street; this perfect, network TV house.

Each night, he picked the lacquered paint off the bench, bit by bit. Was it really ancient? The salesman had told them it was from some Chinese court a thousand years ago but probably they were just young and he was just slick. When you didn't know any better, saying yes was the surest way to seem like you did. That was a lot of their life. We were young; we said yes.

Then one night, one random Wednesday in May, and quite by accident, he saw Ali. She was in her bedroom. She must have just gotten out of the shower. He felt a lightness in his jaw, like blotter paper was pulling away his saliva. She was curvy, counterfactual to the physical world. She was so much that he heard ringing in his ears. White towel bright against perfect skin. She applied something to her legs, dried her hair, a series of products, a holy ministering of lotion and spray. Did he grow hard? Maybe, probably, amazingly, he didn't know. The moment enraptured him. He was outside his body. Uncut lust. Crazy-making. She laid pajamas on her bed. Then she came to the window, and she saw him. They got along well enough. She was funny and self-deprecating. The first to point out that she was from California, an outsider. She was pretty, freckles and brown, wavy hair, and he'd always been a little uneasy around her because of this. Tried to avoid eye contact. But through these windows, the tension was eased and it some-how didn't seem unnatural that he was looking. The glass was a filter, or a protection, or a conversion. Strung tight, a human vibration. He didn't know what had gotten into him, what recklessness or disregard burred from what he had considered, previously, to be a basically smooth and moral soul. He stared back. Then, as if having confirmed his consent, Ali took off her towel. Slowly. She was naked. For him. God, she launched all the ships. He put his fore-head to the glass. TruView window. Employee discount. See a better future. It was cold and smooth and so pure it didn't even catch his breath.

Only then did she close the blinds.

Adam was breathless. Dizzy. Guilty too. *What have I done, what did I see, what have . . .* But not enough to stop himself from urgently masturbating in the upstairs bathroom, finding himself imagining, even more than the parts of her body she had revealed to him, her eyes. Looking into his. It was their world alone within those four borders of the window, behind the screen of glass, a portal as a service. He was the poor man putting up with a postpartum-depression-addled woman who might actually hate him. He needed release. He needed . . . her. An artist, young and hungry. Positive and still going for it, wanting better things. What did he and Sarah know about that? They were just trying to hang on.

And that night, until Maddie screamed at the foot of their bed, until Sarah groaned and stirred, he slept so soundly that the wake up, the sound of his wife and baby, seemed like the intruding dream. His real life was somewhere down, dark and soft, in the place behind his closed eyes. All he wanted was to sleep. To never wake up.

He didn't dare hope it would happen again. But the next night, there she was. And though it made him feel ridiculous, he undressed for her, too. He prayed that she got something from it, but like most prayers, he knew it would go unanswered, so he stopped. This was hers. This was his. It became their ritual. Akin he supposed, though he'd never been addicted to any drug, to what someone might feel anticipating a fix. More urgent than any lusting he'd experienced before. A necessary rebalance of his bodily chemicals. It was a happy arrangement, he thought. He could even make a signal, a small movement of his finger, and she would turn around for him, bend over, squeeze and strut. Through these four corners, through this glass he could do anything . . . he could be anyone . . . it was bliss.

He began following women who looked like Ali on Instagram. Those freckles. That wonderful, zaftig form. It was harmless. Obsessive. Lovely. Pathetic. None of them were her. He couldn't get enough. The more he followed, the more the app suggested he follow. Dancing, slinky ladies in their bedrooms, blowing kisses to him. It was blessed under the Church of Everyone Does It. We were *all* unhealthy in our appetites. What even was social media? If everyone was unhealthy, then nobody was. Or something. It didn't matter. And after he was fired, he relied on this ritual even more. Everything was falling apart, but each night, he had something to get him through. Nothing to harm anyone. Nothing that meant *anything*. A little salve. That's what we're all looking for. Something to get us through to the next day.

Until one night, Sarah came in behind him.

CHAPTER

9

Evie

MAYBE YOU KNOW how it ended with that woman. Of course you have access to that. She never did leave her husband for him. In retrospect, that was a silly thing to expect. But Crispin . . .

In the end, she filed a complaint against him. She said she "felt threatened by his continued and aggressive attention."

Of course I'm using air quotes. It's ridiculous. There was some mix-up about a package, a delivery she claimed had been sent by Crispin that was full of drugs. Trying to get her in trouble. Which is utter horseshit. My son wouldn't hurt anyone. My son has given to the World Wildlife Fund every year since he was five years old. He *cared* about life. And he *cared* about the rules. Why would he go so *far* to fuck up her life? Someone he loved? Where would he even get the drugs? None of it makes sense.

He just cared too much. But that's not a bad thing. It's like I said: the world would be a better place if we all cared as much as my son did.

Next? Well, last week my son's boss called me while I was at work. She wanted to know if Crispin was with me. I told her he wasn't, of course. I told her I was sure he was with her, actually, in Seattle. A Logicstyx come-to-the-mothership bonding experience. As you know, the company is being readied to be acquired. Everyone is about to become God-rich and they wanted to "protect the culture." Kumbaya and kombucha. But, no, his boss said that he hadn't shown up. I wanted to yell at her, to tell you the truth, like she was his teacher and had lost him on a field trip to OMSI. *My son? How have you lost my son!*

Crispin had been dreading the trip for weeks. Everything could have been done online, remote. In fact, the business's entire reason for existence was to enable just such a mode, and still, they *insisted*.

His boss told me that he hadn't shown up to any of the activities, though he was still pushing code to the server and getting his work done (of course, that's my son). He'd skipped the kayaking whale tour *and* the happy hour. He wasn't answering his phone or responding to email, and he still hadn't checked in to the team apartment. She called the Portland offices, but he hadn't been showing up there either. She did this very annoying thing some women do. It was a bit of a story a few years ago, if you remember. Vocal fry. You don't do it, don't worry. It's that white static pop between words. And, like usual, it was accepted, even charming, on men—Ira Glass—but on women—anyone Ira Glass mentored—it was annoying. But I couldn't help it. The more this woman talked, his boss, the more her voice bothered me. *Of course* he was missing kayaking and happy hour, I wanted to shout at her. Would you listen to yourself? He's got more important things to do!

No, I didn't actually say that.

"He's probably working from home," I told her. "After all, code is still being pushed, like you said."

"Yes, of course." She made a *meal* out of that last word. "He *always* gets his work done, but he is usually very prompt in his communications."

"Well, if he's still getting his work done, then maybe it doesn't matter if he shows up for your gather-round circle time meetings," I told her. "Maybe, one supervisor to another, you should just let a good thing go."

I admit I was being snotty, but she was being insufferable and I was *busy*. It was obvious that she was jealous of Crispin. It's pretty common among his bosses and coworkers. He is just so talented that he often doesn't need what they want to teach him.

She seemed taken aback by my bluntness, and I felt sorry about that, obviously, but also a little embarrassed for her. It didn't befit a woman of her title at a big, teeth-out tech start-up. She was showing her belly for a scratch to a pride of lions. She was going to get her intestines ripped out.

Did I tell her about Ali? Is that what she said? I guess I must have. I don't remember it that way though, I just remember saying that perhaps he didn't want to show up because of personal circumstances.

"He might be feeling a little blue," is what I said.

I didn't tell his boss all of the gory details, of course not, I *am not* my mother. I just said Crispin might need some space. And if his work was still getting done, maybe she could give it to him.

"OK," his boss allowed. "As long as the work is getting done."

"Thank you," I told her. "He will be fine in a few days, you'll see."

"Yes, OK, of course. I understand." Blah, blah, blah.

He was the best coder she had on her team. The best coder in the entire company. She needed to believe that he would be OK.

But when I hung up, I knew . . .

Crispin had gotten carried away again.

10

Kemp

THE NEXT TIME he saw her was at the end of the summer and fall coming in fast. It was another event, but this time without the husband. Crispin approached with two beers in hand.

"Hi," he said. "I've got one too many, could you help me?"

She laughed, all her teeth, and he could see sweat in the slope of her neckline. She tilted her head toward the coffee table, and he shrugged.

"No coasters—I'd ruin it forever."

Her boss was watching, so he took her elbow and guided her away, to a back room people rarely found, where the cigars were kept. Each cylinder of expensive tobacco had its own little lit-up bedroom, suspended in environmental purity, perfectly calibrated to keep each cigar pristine. It was grotesque. Of all the ways to use your money. But rich people were like that. *He* would never be like that, he reminded himself again. When he was rich, he would be different. He would act only on feeling, passion, *life*. He would keep in mind that money was boring, that power was a virus.

"We're going to get in trouble," she told him. "I don't think we should be back here."

"Ah," he said with a wink. "I get away with anything in this house."

"Wow," she said, low and slow, like she was a teacher, and he was a cheeky student. "Look at the bad boy."

"I come to a lot of these," he said. "I don't even like them, now that I think of it. It just doesn't feel like I can say no."

"You need to learn how to stand up for yourself."

He was staring at her. He knew he shouldn't be. He couldn't help it.

"Why are you looking at me like that?" she asked. "I saw you looking at me like that last time too. You're far too young to be looking at me like that."

"I'm almost twenty-four," he said, because he was, but also because she had startled him. Oh, he was an idiot. A toddler proudly holding out his chubby fingers to show how many he was. "I'm Crispin. I'm a coder—I work at Logicstyx."

"I know you," she said.

"Do you?"

He hoped she recognized the name of his company too. That alone would be enough to convey that he was on the precipice of wealth. A tightrope. No bragging here, just facts. To be wealthy enough to spurn wealth. Did she see him doing it? Look, no hands!

"Logicstyx at least," she said with a sly look. "The company that will soon be watching me, no matter where I am."

"We're not all bad," he said. "In fact, most people like the convenience."

She laughed. "Sure, Logicstyx is a hot little company these days."

"Not so little anymore," he said, just a touch of bitterness because the company was growing in leaps, bounds, moonshots. Money washing in. Everyone expected to be acquired any day now. His coworkers counted stock options like dragons sitting on their heaps of gold. HR even brought in a counselor of sorts, whose job was to guide the soon-to-be rich. Sudden wealth is apparently a hard transition. *There are many people,* the bearded man told them at an all-hands meeting, speaking in the doleful way of someone who's seen terrible things, *who turn to drugs.*

Crispin's father was the worst. Obsessed with Logicstyx, he began talking to him more than he ever had in the past. Parries Crispin had to fight off. En garde! All growing up, Crispin had almost exclusively talked with his mother. His therapist said in some ways he had become enmeshed. His father, meanwhile, stayed distant. Always busy, always working. Piloting his career as an angel funder with obsession and zeal, constantly jetting off to New York or San Francisco, ceding the nuclear family to mother and son. Now his father didn't seem to recognize, or perhaps didn't care, how transparent his greed was. His ulterior motive neoned. His son worked for a company that he wanted to fund. And so, suddenly, a relationship with his son was something he had to acquire as well. Don't you see that I love you? What a sour thing.

"I heard a big payday is coming for you," she said. "Will you buy a private island, or are you more of a private mountain type?"

"Mountain," he said. "Definitely mountain."

They both laughed, which was delightful in this hushed, low-lit room. It made it seem like they belonged here. Did they belong here? He saw that she was a person who would inhabit wealth beautifully. It would suit her.

"It's just, I'm so busy at work," he said. "And it's starting to feel like there will never be a time I'm not busy, you know?"

It was important, with their age difference, to highlight his upward trajectory. The fact that even though he was young chronologically, by other metrics, he was closer to her. A professional with a bright future but not obsessed with material gain. Well-off but wise. A fine needle, but he was the right kind of thread.

She reached out and touched his palm. Her thumb in the heel of his hand. A soothsayer. What was his future? He felt drawn up, prepared for a big moment.

"Show me something else in this house people don't usually get to see."

"OK," he said. "Come on."

In the upstairs reading room, full of leggy, aquatic light reflected off the koi ponds in the courtyard below, she pushed him hard, in his chest, and told him to sit on the couch. Already, he had no saliva; already he was hard.

She blinked away tears. She looked him in his eyes. She ran her palms up and down her curves and he could hear the rasp of skin against fabric.

"You want to, don't you," she said.

"I—" he started to say, but had to stop, had to swallow. He understood that he shouldn't speak.

"You never will, do you understand?"

She seemed on the edge of something, and already he wanted to save her; already he wanted to push. He slid his hand down, unzipped his pants, and showed her what she had done to him. She reached back and undid her dress; she wasn't wearing a bra. She pulled it over her breasts, revealing one, and then the next. Large, perfect, shadowed and full, each nipple hardening. She went slow. She went so slow. Even though he knew that at any moment someone might come up from the party below, he couldn't tell her to hurry up. Into his head popped the certainty that this moment was kindling into one of the most important of his life. He had no choice but to burn. She tugged the dress down until it hung at her waist and she felt herself. He didn't take his eyes off her. He went harder and harder. She was crying, she was biting her lip, she was sucking tiny dimes of breath as milk leaked from her nipples. He was sick with his desire. He might throw up.

Then she pulled her dress back up; she got herself together.

"What is happening?" he said, trying half a laugh on for size; this was so cruel. He wasn't finished yet.

"I want you to go find something that's theirs," she said. "I want you to find something that is completely theirs and I want you to finish on it, OK? I want you to finish and I want you to think of me."

Then she was gone, and he was unable to do anything but obey. The owners of this house, the insane wealth, it all felt right. He stumbled through empty rooms, half

mad, while the party burbled below. He found the yawn-
ing, cold garage. Luxury cars, parked side by side. He
came onto the hood of a cherry-red Tesla Model X. He felt
disgusting, knotty, and alive. He felt in love.

And as he came, he heard again the words she'd said
to him.

"This will never happen again."

11

Adam

*D*ID HE DO *something, what did he do, did he do* something, what did he do . . .

He picked Maddie up but she cried on. Her gums were red. Were they too red? Was she sick? Then, before he could catch the signs, she spit up on his shoulder, down his front. She was angry. Was she tired? He held her away from him.

"What do you want?" he wondered. "What could you possibly fucking want?"

She cried even harder. Teething? He gave her a twist of wet rag that had been frozen. She wouldn't even open her mouth. He dropped it to the floor.

"I love you!" he said desperately, almost singing it, trying to convince himself. "I love you so much."

He decided to put Maddie down for another nap. It wasn't ideal. Much too late in the day. But sometimes you did things with your kids that weren't ideal. You just needed a moment to go and check that your neighbor hadn't been kidnapped by her ex-boyfriend. It was impossible, it was laughable, it was barnacled at the back of his brain. He just needed to *check*. Scrape the thought off.

He rocked Maddie in the glider, singing "You Are My Sunshine" over and over again. He sang the whole thing. Not just the start, which was tooth-achingly sweet, but the later verses too, which he'd looked up online. He couldn't sing them in front of Sarah anymore. She had stopped him, horror unfolding on her face, forbidding him to continue, as if the lyrics were a spell she'd be cursed under.

"It's so sad," Sarah said. "Can't you just sing the happy part like everyone else?"

Maddie stayed cranky, kept trying to lift her head, but running hot, her impossibly smooth cheeks, easing into it, settling in.

"*You told me once, dear, you really loved me. And no one else could come between. But now you've left me and love another; you have shattered all of my dreams . . .*"

Adam sang, the words written on his heart. The chair had a stain on its arm, who knew from where. Dust bunnies colonized the far corner of the room. The baseboards were filthy. When was the last time they had cleaned their baseboards? What was the point of a newly remodeled home if it was just going to be filthy all the time?

Maddie's face bloomed into a smile and she giggled at something, eyes fluttering like a moth's wings, almost asleep now. Adam was overwhelmed suddenly with love for her. Most of SAHD life was tedious, sometimes unbearable, but there were moments when you knew there wasn't anything else more important than this. Isn't that what they always said? You don't lay on your deathbed and . . . blah, blah, blah. So why was it so easy to forget? Play with his phone. Check the lives of his friends. Refresh job listings. As if he wanted anything but her. Her soft skin, smell of baby shampoo and breast milk. He leaned into her head, her splatter of fine hair, and inhaled. *Remember this*, he told himself, *just remember this*.

When she was asleep, he brought her to her crib, then unwound his spine vertebral disc by disc, the motion creating a fulcrum of his lumbar (really, he should bend his knees, but he wasn't old yet, was he?). It ached, but the reward was worth the cost. Be gentle enough and she would stay asleep. A dandelion fluff, a whisper, a tissue to the floor. He stood up; she stayed sleeping. Huffing dreams. A miracle. Praise be. Again, he was struck by how bad an idea this was. He should just stay here and watch his daughter sleep. This wasn't his problem to get messed up in. If he was really worried, he should call the police. But nothing about this day seemed to be going well, so in the spirit of gamblers everywhere, he doubled down. He turned up the sound machine and crept from the room.

He went outside, locking the door behind him. (Can't have a psycho trying his door at random, running away with his baby.) Down the front three steps and then back up to check that he had, in fact, locked the door. *He had, had he, he had, had he, he had, had he.* Then the thoughts of the stove on or a window open. But he pushed them away. No time for Intrusive Thought Radio. Sarah would be home soon. He felt the agitation of an unchecked tic static his thinking. It would go away if he pressed on. Throw to commercial break. This was a transition. Transitions were the worst, and soon enough, he'd be into something new.

He looked down the street and saw his neighbor Charlie, a yarny naturopath who was constantly boiling, slicing, pressing various roots, seeds, and leaves. She was in front of her house, talking with Tin Can Sam, the homeless man (houseless? Person without a home?) who collected their cans and bottles every Wednesday.

There was no way Adam could get across the street without Charlie seeing him. And if she saw him, she would tell Sarah. *Your husband is sniffing around Ali's house again . . .*

Disaster, radiation, weeks of stink.

Charlie hated Adam. After Sarah caught him at the window, she ran to Charlie. There she stayed, late into the night, drinking wine. She came home and whisper-shouted at him. A fight that started with his misstep *(But nothing actually happened!)* and ballooned bigger and bigger until it held foundational problems *(Do you even love me anymore? You're so bleak! You just scroll your phone! I feel like I'm constantly letting you down!)* Again, she'd stormed off, and Adam was left thinking about the question she had asked him once: *Do you ever think about stepping in front of busses?*

Later, she came home, well past one in the morning, face wet, and they had sex for the first and last time since Maddie. A slow, careful, intense series of questions and answers that left him suspecting he had just done something he should feel guilty about. Worse than before. Was life just always worse and worse than before?

"Is this how you like it?" she kept wondering.

"Yes," was the only thing he was allowed to say.

And although they hadn't slept together since, and Sarah still wasn't back to her old self, she managed a busy, slightly manic simulacrum. For all the soggy heart-to-hearts with Charlie, the counseling session, it had been catching *him* playing Peeping Tom that seemed to set things in motion.

Adam had a thought: if he could take Sam off Charlie's hands, she would go back inside to her boil, boil, toil and trouble, and leave the street unwatched. Then he could check on Ali and be back inside well before Sarah returned home.

"Hey, Sam," he said, walking down the sidewalk. "How's business?"

Sam was basically harmless, muttering to himself each Wednesday as he trundled along, harvesting their aluminum and glass, but he was also, recently, prone to loud bouts of shouting "peanut butter cunt!" to the collective wince of everyone in the neighborhood. Adam didn't think he was dangerous but Sarah, and especially Charlie, had the opposite mindset. *Smoke and fire,* was how Charlie put it once. *And that guy has a lot of smoke.*

"Oh, hello!" Charlie said, and he could see her quick mental math. Adam was detestable, to be sure, but no hater of cunts, peanut butter or otherwise.

"Hello," Sam said, in that oddly formal way he had, almost British. "You've caught us in a bit of a debate."

"A *political* debate," Charlie said, shooting Adam a look that clearly meant *be careful.* Or maybe it was, *you've got to listen to this.*

"My competition," Sam said.

"The other people collecting cans," Charlie clarified.

"Those bums," Sam said. "Are too lazy. Parasites."

His glasses were fogging up. He was wearing an enormous mesh-backed trucker hat for a towing company that promised, *We'll get you out of the Shit!*

"Oh," Adam said.

"So he voted red," Charlie said.

"He's a winner," Sam said. "He's what we need. This is the greatest country in the world because you can get *anything* if you're willing to *work* for it. No handouts."

Charlie shifted her weight, foot to foot, struggling between disgust for this person and a liberal guilt at not being more compassionate for someone in an obviously impossible situation. Her ideals and reality butting heads.

"Right," Adam said. "MAGA."

"MAGA!" Sam said.

"But by now," Adam pointed out, the light goldening, afternoon ticking steadily into the evening hour, "wouldn't you say your competition might be getting a jump on *you*?"

"Right!" Sam said. "Can't have that, can I? Me and the peanut butter cunt, up early, rise and shine!"

"Jesus, Sam," Adam said, but the man didn't seem to notice his rebuke, already huffing off, a bag in each hand.

"Thanks," Charlie said. "I didn't know how to get rid of him. That was . . . that was like magic."

"No problem," Adam said.

She smoothed down her gray apron. Neither of them knew how to act around each other.

"Where's Maddie?"

"Sleeping," he said. "Down for the count. One of those days. I'll probably be up all night with her again."

Charlie laughed. She had a daughter in high school, a junior, who spent most of her time at her father's house. Charlie turned to jelly whenever she saw Maddie. She liked to remind Adam, back when she was still talking to him, not to take this for granted. Everyone and everything was telling him not to take this for granted!

"I could give you some valerian root, maybe a little passionflower?" Charlie said. "It would help." She was forever offering her wares, and it was never clear if she expected payment. It made Adam very uncomfortable.

"No, I think it will be alright," he said, turning away, but Charlie made a small noise, a *hep* sound, like she wanted to say something but couldn't without his help. He turned back. Sarah was probably going to be home in twenty minutes or less. He would have checked her location on his phone, but of course it would only respond with an error. After she'd caught him at the window, actually pushing him to the side and glaring out at Ali, she'd revoked his permissions. Now it was only *she* who was capable of tracking *him*.

"I don't know," Charlie said. "It's . . . it's probably better if I just keep quiet. It's really none of my business."

She wanted him to insist. To pry. He would insist. He would pry. He didn't have time for anything else. The sooner she said whatever it was she wanted to say, the sooner he could get on with it.

"I have Maddie, and I better . . ."

"I saw Tina poking around your house," Charlie said.

"Oh, I'm sure it's nothing," Adam said.

"You don't do drugs, do you, Adam?" Charlie said. "I mean, is Sarah OK?"

Tina was about Adam's age and lived across the street from Charlie in a small, tidy house she obsessed over. She'd grown up in that house, inherited it from her father, and never left. Now it was the site of a constant string of visitors, and, if neighborhood rumors were true, the hub of a minor drug dealing concern.

"We're fine," Adam said.

"It's no business of mine," Charlie said. "I just don't want to see anyone get hurt, and, I'm sorry, but Tina is bad news."

Apart from Tina's alleged illicit activities, Charlie held her in particular contempt because of her floodlight. Any movement from a creature bigger than a cat spotlit Tina's house, but the light, as Charlie liked to constantly complain to them, banked into her bedroom windows, waking her up at all hours.

"I'll . . . keep an eye out," Adam said. "But I'm sure it was nothing. Tina probably just wanted to borrow something. Maybe tools? She's been working on something in her house. I think she might be prepping it to paint."

"She's always working on something," Charlie said. She had moved into the neighborhood a decade before and began her stalemate with Tina shortly thereafter.

"OK, then," Adam said. "Take care."

He started back to his house, shuffling along, listening for the slap of Charlie's screen door. When he heard it, he darted across the street and ducked behind the enormous laurel that grew wild, almost two stories high, on the side of Ali's house. The tree held him in cold shadow with the smell of damp earth. He stayed within its hem, breathing a few moments. He looked up to the second window, the side window into Ali's room. It was open. That was odd, right? The weather was a soggy, punched-through fall muck. Their house didn't get much heat. A single heating output for the whole house was in the living room floor and wheezed a stale slickered ghost that moved anemically and never bothered to linger. Ali had complained about it. Bad insulation. She was always cold. In fact, he and Sarah had given her an old space heater last winter. No way the window should be open.

"Fuck it," he said, foreseeing the loop he was about to enter. *(Should I do something, what should I do, should I . . .)* He shorted the circuit on the thought by jumping into action. He climbed into the laurel tree, branch after branch, leaves falling away, the whole thing trembling. He kept going. A rising feeling to the mouth, dry tongue. Swallow, swallow, swallow. Ice in his stomach, fingers remembering what it was like to climb. He used to be good at this. Good for something. And he pulled himself even with the window. Her bed sat empty, sheets tangled, duvet slumped to the floor. And at first he couldn't decide what he was seeing. A streak, a discoloring. He leaned in closer—it was mud. Ali's bed was covered in mud.

He slipped and fell through the tree, spat out onto the gravel drive, a compaction of bone, his breath driven free. Something fell through the air after him, flutter and swing, and landed on his stomach. An asphalt shingle. A gray asphalt shingle.

The sky was falling.

CHAPTER

12

Sarah

SARAH ARRIVED HOME and there was Adam, standing across the street, on the sidewalk, holding a shingle in his hands and looking dumbly up at Ali's house. Ali's house. Ali's fucking house. Weren't they *done* looking at Ali's house? She wished the entire thing would just implode in dust and sound. Then maybe they could *get past* it all. Shouldn't Adam know better? She had hoped. Oh, God, how she had hoped, but what does hope care? The most flaky companion. If you wanted something to happen, you needed a more reliable verb. Work. You had to *work* for it. She knew that. But did he?

Obviously not.

Him and his obsession with that odd, over-the-top girl. Someone so *different* from them. From her. Young and untethered. Sarah could never be that again, but was that what Adam wanted? As if her plate weren't already full, she had to deal with *this*. Did he know how stupid he came off? Watching a woman undress across the street like some frathouse bro.

"What are you doing?" she said.

"It fell," he said, idiotically.

"Let's *not* start worrying about her roof too," Sarah said. The last thing she wanted just then was to sit through another briefing with her husband about the current state of his guilt surrounding whatever *that* had been with Ali. She had other things to deal with.

"No, I was just worried because, last night . . ."

Was Adam having a stroke? Surely, he was too young to have a stroke. Or maybe that was a heart attack. Maybe strokes didn't care how young you were.

Unbidden to Sarah's mind came a song she'd once been made to remember in Bible study. Six? Seven years old? Something she'd sing to her parents to the great delight of whichever musty, buttoned-up, believing couple they'd invited over for dinner.

If I had a little white box, I'd put Jesus in. I'd take him out and kiss his face and put him right back in. If I had a little black box, I'd put the devil in. I'd take him out and SMACK HIM UP and put him right back in.

The song had always confused her. Why keep the devil with you at all? But now she knew she had just been too young. Now she knew that you kept the devil with you always, inside your deepest, darkest wishes, fears, and fantasies.

"See, the thing is," he continued. "I saw Kemp last night, and he peed. He peed on their house. It was so strange, and I got worried. Because Ali never showed up for work, and Kemp . . . his truck is still here. I was afraid something had happened. It seemed like he was sending a message."

"You were watching?" Sarah said. She remembered Evie's question. Had she seen Crispin recently? She cast about, trying to suss out what she could say, how she could explain it. "He's her *boyfriend*. He had to piss. What's the big deal?"

Did Adam know?

"But they broke up," Adam said, dumbly. "He shouldn't be here, but—Listen, the *way* he held his . . ." Adam cast about in front of his crotch with his hand.

"You're talking about his penis?"

"It was like he was trying to send a message," Adam said. "Like he was trying to tell her that he owned her or something. Like a dog marking his territory."

Jesus. Sarah looked at Kemp's black 4Runner. Tinted windows, impossible to see inside. It was right there, smack in the middle of their street. When was the last time they had been completely honest with each other? *I could never lie to you*, she'd told Adam so often. *I'm so bad at it!* But she lied to him constantly. As much as she lied to herself. Just being nice to him, wasn't even that a little untrue?

"They probably got back together," Sarah said. "I don't want to talk about it."

Then, like two pieces of the night ascending to pull down the rest of the curtain, crows flew from Ali's roof, cawing raucously down at them (stupid humans, cemented to earth), and she shivered. She hated crows. They were of another era. The middle ages. Plague and crusade. She'd read that they were smart, and this made her hate them all the more. Intelligent eyes in the sky. A friend told her once that if you were a bad mother in Germany, they called you a raven mother. And it seemed to fit. The only thing worse than a raven was a crow. Gathered, they were a *murder*, for god's sake.

"The roof is going to be fine, Adam."

"No," he said, a little shaky, looking at her, searching within her, and Sarah didn't like it. She felt handled by this stare, like it was the end of a long night out and he'd had too much to drink and screw civility. He was going to really let her have it. Would she be able to stand when it all came at her? She wasn't sure.

"It's going to be *fine*," she said again.

"But the shingle. What made the shingle fall?"

"Pull it together," she said.

She swallowed; she needed to reset. Try harder. Take a step to the side. This wasn't Adam's fault. Except for watching Ali undress in the window and that shit at his job. So, *actually* it *was* his fault. A little or all. From now until eternity. She was the faulted party and he was the faulter. *Remember that*, she told herself. *Remember who started this.* He'd taken the mantle of fucked up men everywhere and ran.

Sarah grabbed the shingle out of his hands and tossed it on the sidewalk. She would have to try something else. *Remember the feeling from last night, she told herself.* The clarity that had zapped into her as she looked at their darkened house, the whole street quiet, and knew. *You are who I want.*

She stepped toward him, close to his chest, and smelled the Old Spice he'd been wearing since at least the day they met in college.

"I love you so much," she said as she felt his arms tighten around her. It wasn't enough. She wished he would squeeze tighter, show her his strength, and take away her breath. *How much do you love me? How much do you punish me?* Until her breath came in shallow whispers, until *he* was all there was. *Show me. Prove it. Crush me. Do anything.* She wanted to tell him to go tighter and tighter. She wanted to implicate them both into a more powerful and dangerous love. *Do* everything, *Adam*. There was *so much* going on. And for a moment, she thought he'd read her mind. His pectorals flexed, his biceps contracted up against his sweatshirt, the soft scratch of his whiskers.

But he released and stepped away.

"You're doing great," she said, but she couldn't meet his eyes. She was crying. Big, pregnant drops. "I love you, and I don't know if I tell you that enough, but you're doing an amazing job. And I know it's been difficult. I know . . ." She breathed in deeply and rubbed her face hard. "God, I know *I've* been difficult. But we'll get through this. I'll do whatever it takes to get through this. I need you to know that I will do *whatever* it takes."

"It was the *way* he looked," Adam said, stuck on a single idea, like always. His looping thoughts. "The *way* he peed. It was like he was sending a message."

13

Kemp

B UT OF COURSE it did happen again, just like he knew it would. Only a few days after that party, only a few days after he'd deposited himself on that alien shine of the Tesla, they began sleeping together. How did he get her email? It was easy. Google.

Don't write me here, she responded.

Then give me a number, he dashed back.

So they started texting, and then meeting up, and then . . .

Theirs were jagged, startling trysts that tore out the ceiling of what the world could be. Heaving meetings during her lunch (only thirty minutes!) in the park, in the bathroom of a coffee shop, in his car. It was like she was an algorithm solving for his inputs, executing possibilities he'd never imagined before, but once they happened, knew he'd always desperately wanted. Of course he had. He had been so stupid before! She called the shots, and he was happy, no, thrilled to be told what to do. The exact opposite of work. The sexiest thing imaginable.

Then he told her of his house, the house he'd bought just in case . . . no pressure . . . The place that sat empty and paid for, near her work, so convenient, a credit on his account. So sometimes she would text him to be there at a certain time, naked. And he would wait, anticipation growing within him, a torture so pure and powerful that if he looked at it directly, he was sure he would die. What could this mean? What did this say about him? Was he pitiful or passionate? He waited until she finally showed up, always on her schedule, always when she deemed it safe. He never resented her. Love didn't resent. Love accepted. The ugly, the bare, the imperfect. And he was beginning to understand: *this* was love.

Afterward, she would tell him about her family, about her marriage, about the shifting sandbars and currents of her sleep-deprived life with a baby and a frustrated husband. She was always running aground. She was always wrecking, no matter how carefully she charted her course. He was her release valve. A temporary safe passage. And that was all he could be. Nothing more.

"And you're OK with that, Crispin?"

"I'm the happiest I've ever been," he insisted.

But was he? Her ring had disappeared in Costa Rica and she'd never gotten another. That *had to* mean something. Because whenever she did finally arrive, he would be trembling with feeling, a tuning fork vibrating hard enough to twist apart. He had never felt like this before in his life. He would do whatever it took to keep it with him.

So one afternoon he asked, "Would you, I don't know, would you say this is something more? Something that has the potential to be more?"

He was lying in the plush, fuzzy afterward light, naked and spent. He buried his face in the crook of his elbow, smelling his own body odor. He felt like a kid on the high dive board who'd just jumped. That thrill wrapped about his guts. A tightening ribbon of what-would-happen?

She didn't answer, and Crispin took her silence to be a rallying within her, building up the strength to say something she shouldn't. It was scary to jump. He understood that. But what a view once you did. What a rush.

Deep breath. *It is worth it!* He thought at her. *Don't you see how this will be worth it?*

"I'm married," she said. "I have a—"

"I know, I know," he said. "But that doesn't scare me, I've always wanted this."

"What do you think *this* is?" she said.

"A family," he told her.

He would do anything for her. Just a week into their . . . arrangement, Crispin had coded a bot to push out his work on randomized deadlines days in advance, simulating his presence. It even drafted work-specific replies to incoming emails. Vague, but authentic-seeming. He had enough clout at Logicstyx that they all read more meaning than was actually there into anything he did. On it or you'll have it EOD. He did his actual work late into the night, cashing Red Bulls and filling the trash can with pistachio shells. That way, during the day, he was free to wait for her. Available whenever she wanted him. It was a lot of work, but it was worth it. She was worth it.

"These things aren't easy," he said.

"These things?" she looked at him, eyes wet with feeling. To stop those tears. How could anyone who knew the whole story think what he was doing with her was wrong? He was giving her another option. An escape route.

"Unhappy marriages," he said. "And, you know, it won't get better. It never does. My parents, they stay together, and they shouldn't. It's not good. It's not good for anyone."

"Don't talk about my marriage," she said and began to gather her clothing. Their rendezvous, full of urgency, were heavy doors pushed open by some natural force he didn't understand. The moment she arrived, the door began closing again. Once it shut, she would give him nothing until whatever force was behind her visits blew it open again.

"Is there anything in you," he whispered. "Anything that makes you think this is more than just . . . ?"

"I have a family," she told him again. "I have a child. You knew what this was when it started. I thought that was part of the appeal. No strings attached. Isn't that some kind of porn fantasy you men have?"

"Porn fantasy?" Is that what she thought they were doing? That was *not* what they were doing. Yes, the sex was scream-out-good, yes, he loved to see her claw marks down his shoulder blades the next day, but, no, it wasn't like some free clip on Pornhub.

He took a deep breath. He felt the urge to grip all the harder, but fought it. Knew from past experience that you couldn't trust your urges in some cases. That sometimes people took his insistence, his dedication, his passion, as something else. He needed to play this just right.

"I know, I know, I know," he said, putting a smile on his words. "But this doesn't seem like anything else that I've been in before. Is there anything to that? Or am I making it up? Because, if I am, that's cool, just shoot me now, OK?" He laughed at himself and then tilted his face up, looked into her brown eyes, sheened with what he was heartened to see were tears. Pale skin, black hair. Maybe he'd played this just right after all.

"We need to stop this," she said. "Just—it's only been a couple weeks, Crispin. A just-for-fun thing. And now it's over."

"No," he pleaded. This was going wrong. How was this going so wrong? He needed more time. He was so good at everything else, so how could this one thing, this most important thing, be so hard? Again and again, he failed. He wanted to scream until his throat was tattered, until his lungs gave out.

"Stay," he said.

"It *is* just for fun," he said.

"Do you want a tea?" he said.

He'd long ago stocked the kitchen with every single kind he could find. Cabinets and cabinets of fragrant, dried leaves. The very best stuff imported from far off places at ridiculous prices. One of them, the Da Hong Pao, had roots so deep it tickled the Ming Dynasty. The stuff went for $600,000 a pound!

"I promise you," he said. "I'm fine with it just being whatever. I was just thinking out loud. It was stupid. Sometimes I don't know why I say the things I do. It gets me in trouble. I self-sabotage. This is just for fun. Let's keep it just for fun. It's really hot like this; you're right."

"Not anymore," she said. "Maybe it's time for me to be better. And you too, Crispin. You could do so much better." She gestured around. Empty house, quiet street, humming refrigerator keeping nothing but bachelor air crisp and cold. "You shouldn't be alone."

Later, Crispin lay alone in the darkness of his room, only the traffic lights from 50th bouncing in like lost fireflies, and looked at her husband on Instagram, Twitter, Facebook. The broad, smiling face, the thin shoulders, the lanky build. Down, down, down he went, following this man, this stranger, to see where, exactly, he'd become the man that deserved everything that should have been Crispin's.

PART 2
The Girl Across the Street

Getting to be too much

There's something that's been bugging me about Mr. Handsome. He's over here, and he's into me, he's into *it*, or otherwise, he's on his computer, doing his work (big-shot coder at a tech company you would DEFINITELY know), or he's at my window. It's like he's keeping watch, waiting for something. It's hard to know. But it's been bothering me because it's hard to know *anything* with him. He's always got his plans. And it's complicated. Like, he helped me out, in a big way, and it sort of funds his influence over what we got going on. Only it can't be just for him either, because I like it too, don't I? He's just getting a little too much lately. And that shit with my window, always going there and looking out. I don't like it. I don't like it one bit. I *know* that window.

POSTED BY UNKNOWN AT 6:17 PM
0 COMMENTS:

CHAPTER

14

Adam

ADAM IN COLLEGE. How to describe it? Adored. Special. A mascot. The party where he met Sarah was in a big, shaggy living room universally envied for the space it provided friends and strangers to get drunk and high and make the kind of memories they would warn their kids about in twenty years. Safety first. Adam was a little stoned, sure, but leaning into the role, playing it bigger, hoping people would notice. Scooting from one obliging girl to the next, he asked for head rubs. And they had him. Welcomed him between their knees to touch his scalp. He felt their warmth through the denim covering their thighs. *He's so high*, they kept telling each other, giving permission to him and themselves to do what they were doing. *Look at him, he's on the moon!* He was adopted by all. Could be their child or their lover. So adorably hapless. He was Adam. Beautiful Adam. Literally the face of June for a calendar he and some of the other guys who hung out at the rock wall had put together to raise funds. Not even for something charitable. No feed-the-orphans for them. It was a weeklong camping trip to Yosemite. Ripped Rock Rats. Get yours today. Though, being climbers, they were not exactly ripped. More like *preserved*, Sarah told him later. Sticks of beef jerky. Sinewy and long.

"Yum-yum," Adam had said.

Still, the calendars sold out. Still, they were forgiven. Those *boys*.

So head rub, head rub, head rub. Rub head. Until he got to Sarah, who said, "Who are you, and when was the last time you washed this beaver pelt?"

Romantic first words? They were something else. Still, for Adam, it was over.

He found out that she liked her legs but hated her hands. She rode her bike with her headphones in, listening to Langhorn Slim and other singers from a playlist she named *The Hope Peddlers*. She put sunblock on her nose. Mint chocolate was her favorite. She had theories about educational best practices. She used to go to church. She soaked beans overnight in big cloth-covered bowls for soups that had French names. They drove to the coast together, just the two of them. They sat in the roaring darkness on gray sand and pointed out which driftwood looked like what monsters.

He told her his deepest secret. She hadn't even asked.

"You have thoughts?" she clarified, but not like she was confused or scared. More like she was turning out the lights at the restaurant they both worked at after a long day. She wanted to be sure she got every last one.

"Sometimes . . . sometimes they won't leave me alone," he said. "Just little things get in. Not like I want to *do* any of them. Just, you know, *things*. Images. Situations."

"What kinds of situations?"

"I don't even know," Adam said. He paused for a long, thin moment. A reedy blade of grass. Cut or sting, depending on what you did with it. What to tell her . . . A little of the truth? Half of the truth? The whole goddamn thing? He'd never told anyone even a fraction. Anything would be everything. It was a cup within him that he'd been balancing—don't spill a drop—for how long? His jaw hurt from clenching his teeth. A roil and roll within him, he couldn't place where, only something had come loose.

"OK, it's like this," he said. "The first time it ever happened—well, I guess, the first time I can *remember* it happening, I was with my dad. We were in the basement, and he was looking for something. He was on his knees, and I saw how at the back of his head, he had a bald spot. Of course I knew he was going bald, but, like, it was bigger than I thought it would be? And there was this sledgehammer lying there? There were a bunch of other tools too, but I just fixated on the sledgehammer. And I saw that bald spot, and all I could think about was what it would look like if the sledgehammer hit it."

No, even this wasn't quite right. Adam had come this far, so he pushed himself to go all the way. Damn the cup. Damn the water. It was raining now. Fine curtains of mist closing in on them. The blasted, blackened tree trunk, roots and all, gaping at his side, feeling as if it would swallow him whole. The ocean roared titanically. Wetness touched his face, tissues layering, one after the next. Soon he'd be covered whole.

"I kept imagining swinging that sledgehammer into his head."

Hiss and shush. Bright cold. He clenched and
unclenched his fists. Sand between his wiggling toes. Currents of ice. He felt his right forearm. He was proud of
the hard muscle there. He'd come to college having never
had a girlfriend, the body of a pale Gumby, not being particularly known, one way or the other, as this or that, but
now . . .

"It's not like I wanted to kill him or hurt him. It was
just like . . . I was scared of myself for even having the
thought? Like, because I was having the thought, then it
would happen, whether I liked it or not? And I was so
worried, you know? I was so worried that I was a monster?
Like one of those Columbine boys, or whatever? I kept
telling myself, stop thinking about this. Just stop. But
the more I tried to stop, the more it kept coming. It's that
purple cow thing. Don't think of a purple cow! And, of
course, that's all you think about. So, sometimes I get in
these, like, loops?"

"Oh, Adam," she said.

"I would never do it," he said. "Of course I would never
do something like that. It's just . . . Like violent thoughts.
They were hard. They were . . ."

"And you still have them?" Sarah wondered. "These
intrusive thoughts?"

"Sometimes," he said. Intrusive thoughts. She had a
term. And just having that term did something for him.
He looked down at his feet squelching back and forth.
Down, down, down into the sand. Was she worried for her
safety now? They had driven out here in her tiny Yaris. If
she felt too scared of him, how would he get back? Hitch-
hiker. Bus rider. Highway man disappeared.

She put a hand out and touched his knee.

"That sounds really hard," she said. "That sounds really scary."

Adam took in a long, shaky breath, and he cried into his hands. He'd spent so many of his years holding back from himself. A flush of love released within him that was obsessive in its own right. He felt so protected under her palms that he knew he would do the same for her. See her totally, accept whatever that meant.

The whole way home, Adam driving this time and Sarah asleep in the passenger seat, Elliott Smith and a persistent, dogging moon, he kept thinking how easy it would have been for him to not go to that party, or for her. How there were a million worlds where they never met each other, and he closed his eyes and clenched his teeth. He checked that she was still there next to him. And again. Then one last time to be sure. Because that was love.

*   *   *

Adam stood, holding the shingle. Gray, overcast day. Rough on his hands. Veined with moss as though it had once been a part of something alive. A dragon's scale. It was stupid to still be holding it, incriminating even. But stupidity never does preclude action, Adam was well aware. In fact, oftentimes, just before he did something stupid, a small, white, fizzy space opened before him. Almost a whimsy. It existed without tense. Not in the present or future. Not yet. And he could stunt there, within it, for eons. A strange serum to his monkey thinking. Damn the consequences. But then, if he *did* choose to jump into the foamy waters, to click the link, to say the thing, to watch the girl across the street, to stand and hold the shingle, to take the phone call, then everything collapsed and he was stuck with himself again.

And still he held. Because why the shingle? Why the shingle?

The shingle seemed important. All the times he'd obsessed over a stove left on or a door unlocked, and now, here, it was real. Something *had* happened. One of his small fears hadn't been coddled enough and it had grown big, fearsome, and hungry.

The muddy disarray of Ali's room, the hurried, messy chaos, confirmed his fears. Violence had been done. Then, climbing back down, he'd slipped on something and there it was. A shingle. Why was there a shingle in the laurel? Wind storm? Squirrels?

Sarah ripped the shingle out of his hands, and he was glad for it. He was unsure he could have managed to let go on his own.

"Do you know that?" she wondered. "Do you know I would do anything for you?"

Her words were too loud, too many, too much.

"Stop talking," he told her, though he could barely manage. Something was coming to him, and it was squiggly with slime, hard to hold on to, but alive and twisting. "Just shut up and stop talking."

She turned and left him, went into the house, a heavy storm in the hunch of her shoulders. Then she returned, furious, shouting that his phone was ringing, that the door had been locked, that Maddie was wailing. Everything she said came through distorted, a squelch of misaimed feeling. He shouldn't have answered the call. He should have ignored it and asked his wife what the fuck was going on. But he *had* to answer it. It might *be* something.

He took the phone.

"Great, and just take the call while I go take care of our baby."

"You know what?" Adam said, phone still jiggling in his hand. "You always say how much you like this little life we have, but that's because Maddie's some decoration to you. Go take her off the shelf. Go actually *play* with her. Go feed her."

He turned his back on his wife. He closed his eyes and waited for the door to slam behind him. Sarah's expression flashed into his mind even though he couldn't see it. A magic trick couples can do. Imagine the very worst from their partner. Look, no hands. He was good at it.

"Hello?" he said.

"Adam?"

"Yes?"

"This is Candice. I work with Ali? I think you called earlier?"

"Oh." He pulled the phone away from his ear, numbers ticking upward, timing his call, red background, a flashing, urgent thing. *What did he do, did he do something, what did he . . .* "Sorry about that, but how did you get my number?"

"Ali has you listed as a contact in her file. You're an emergency contact."

"Oh," Adam said. He was? He couldn't believe it. Emergency contact was for family or significant others. He wasn't those things . . . was he?

"What's going on?" he demanded.

"She never came in today," Candice said. "She didn't even call. I'm worried."

Adam looked up at Ali's roof, then over to Kemp's SUV. Shouldn't he have left by now? Weren't they broken

up? Ali and Kemp had broken up. He could feel Sarah
watching him through the windows, so he began walking down Salmon Street toward César Chávez Boulevard.
Cracks in the sidewalk there—don't step on them and
break someone's back. Over their mulched tree lawn blan-
keted by rotting leaves. Out across their street. Didn't look
for traffic, a sixth sense, didn't need to.

"She never came in today?" Adam said, repeating,
repeating, repeating. It was one thing to fantasize, but this
was . . .

Ali had never gone into work. That was a fact.
She never went in, she never called, and she wasn't in
her room—which was now a mess, with the window
open and mud everywhere. And Kemp's truck was still
there. Another fact. What did those make when added
together? He remembered Ali's uneasiness in the grocery
store. How Kemp had been "too much." So, he of the
tech-start-up golden ticket couldn't handle being told
no. Had he rented a car, hidden his tracks, taken her
against her will?

"And she got this package," Candice said. "And . . . I
opened it. We do that sometimes for each other. Like, if I'm
at lunch when a new pair of boots comes in, or whatever,
she'll open them and text me pictures of my boots and say
funny things about how they like me more than her."

"OK."

"We have the same size."

"What the fuck is going on?"

"I'm sorry, that doesn't really matter."

Adam stopped, looked back down the street. His
house, red paint, white fence, new but made to look clas-
sic. An American dream. They were paying for it. Maybe

always would be. What had been comfortable with both of them working was a stretch on just Sarah's salary. And across the street, Ali's place, ramshackle, easily the worst in the neighborhood—where was she? Crows gathering on the eaves, more and more of them. He turned and kept walking, faster now, around the block and onward.

"So, what?" Adam said, trying to sound annoyed. "You opened some, like, fuzzy handcuffs or something?"

"Listen, they have these little feet stamped into them. Like bird feet."

"What are you talking about? What has bird feet?"

"They're pills. It's an entire box of pills. I think they're ecstasy pills? At least, that's what Google thinks they are."

"OK . . ." Adam shivered inwardly.

"Did you know Ali did ecstasy?" Candice wondered.

"No," he said.

"It's just . . . like, she doesn't show up to work, then a strange package arrives, and it's full of drugs? Like, that's kind of fucked up, you know?"

"Maybe she's out?" Adam said, carefully. "On a vision quest?"

"A vision quest?"

"I don't know, what do people do with ecstasy?"

"They dance. And don't you think she would take the drugs with her, if that's what they were for?"

"That's true," he allowed, mind scrambling, searching for a way out.

"And there were other pills too," she said.

"Other pills? Like *other* drugs?"

"Yeah, I think some of them are oxy, but I swear to God, there's this shit with skull and crossbones on it that I think is actual fucking poison."

"Well, that's not . . . There's no way there would be poison. Why would she have poison?"

"It came with instructions."

"The ecstasy?"

"The poison! The poison came with instructions. There are tables on the right dosages for body type. It's called Bonze. I looked it up on Silk Road." A fumble in the receiver and then harsh, whispered words: "That shit is cyanide."

"This doesn't make any sense. That's not right."

"She's not trying to kill herself," Candice said. "Right? That's not what this is about. Everything's going so well for her now."

Her art. Her moving on from Kemp. It *had* all been going well for her. Now he imagined her being taken somewhere by Kemp. Just as life was turning around for her. He was vibrating. Numb fingers from holding a power tool too long. But that's how it went, right? That's why they were called tragedies. Adam thought about her most recent Instagram post. The dark figure in the square of light. It had been him. A presence reigning over her from the window across the street. How embarrassing. Was it obvious to anyone else? They hardly talked in real life, but there he'd been, watching her from the window. The window across the street. A call for help? Her version of the Bat-Signal? And what had he done? He had a connection with her through glass, but in real life? In real life, he'd done nothing. He was *still* doing nothing.

"You're right," he said. "She definitely wasn't planning . . . But, hey, why don't you just throw the box away, OK? It was probably just sent to her by mistake. Like, if it really is what you think it is, then it's probably not safe to be handling it. Just throw it away, and do her a favor."

"But here's the really fucked up thing, OK?" Candice's voice dropped even further, and Adam stopped walking. He felt a little sick; a tangle in his gut. "The really fucked up thing is that there's no return address, but there *is* a sticker on it. From Logicstyx."

"Oh . . ." Adam said.

"It's like this tech company," she said.

"Right."

"Listen, Ali was under a lot of pressure lately because aside from that commission to do all those T-shirts? And this other thing for Mel Sweetney? There was this guy, her ex-boyfriend, and he was . . . Well, he would just show up. And he has been doing it more and more."

"Kemp," Adam said.

"Yeah," Candice said. "Right, but did you know this fucker works at Logicstyx?"

"So what, he was going to—"

"He was trying to fuck with her life, you know? And if he was willing to go that far, send a bunch of illegal things to Ali's work, just because she broke up with him, how much more would he do?"

"What are you saying?"

"Where *is* Ali, is what I'm saying. She just up and disappears and then gets a box of drugs from Kemp? This shit is not adding up. I think *I have to* call the cops, right? I mean, if they can dust this shit for fingerprints, then maybe they can link it to Kemp. And her most recent blog posts, I mean, it's a little creepy, I'm not going to lie."

"Her blog?"

"Her Internet diary, or whatever. She calls him Mr. Handsome on there, but he's been acting creepier and creepier. He fucked up her knee the other day trying to, like, grab her!"

"I think you should just throw that package away," Adam said, really shaken now, desperate. The skin on the back of his neck seemed to be inching toward his skull. He hunched up, tightening his shoulders, the pop and fizz in the back of his thinking. *What did he do, did he do something, what did he do, did he do something, what did he . . .*

"—shit, my boss, gotta go."

"Throw it away," he shouted into the phone, but the call was already dead. "Throw it away, please!" He was almost crying. He could see his life slipping away. It had been such a stupid idea. Childish and petty. Because if anyone dusted that box, all they would find were his own fingerprints.

15

Evie

WHAT DO YOU mean how would I characterize my relationship with Sarah Cooper? I was her boss, and she was my employee. That's it. Maybe it doesn't look like the boss-subordinate dynamic typical in a corporate environment, but of course it wouldn't, would it? In a school setting, relationships get a little more . . . intense. And that opens up opportunities for bonding. That's to be expected. You don't fault the boys at war for making brothers in the trenches. You applaud it.

I tell my husband all the time that we're not a bunch of IT consultants. We don't finish a task and strike it from the list. We don't meet up for happy hour once a month and sign birthday cards. Of course we do all of that too. But this is so much *more*. This is teaching. These are *kids* we are working with. *This* work is never done because *they* are never done. They *always* need more. It creates heat, a greenhouse. Things grow. They always do. Attachments, dependencies, friendships. Every year, there is something new that creeps in that maybe shouldn't, like English ivy. But it's harmless. Nine times out of ten, it's completely harmless.

To imply that I made a pass at Sarah? That devalues our hard work. That's just so typical of the patriarchy, I'm sorry, but it is. You of all people should recognize that.

No, I don't think you understand. Sarah was under a lot of stress. She wasn't acting like she normally would. She wasn't thinking straight.

I always say teachers are modern-day saints. We sure as hell don't do it for the money. What other profession literally touches every single person in the nation? Medical, maybe, and you don't expect doctors to be half-assed. You wouldn't question the long hours if I was wearing a white coat. We're doing the most important work you can do.

What does this have to do with Crispin, anyway?

If you're wondering about the texts and the gifts, look, there is always a teacher that needs a little bit more. Recently, it's been Sarah. I've developed an instinct for when a teacher needs a little bit more. And she was struggling. If I can reach out before it gets too hard, I can make life easier for both of us. I could see she was putting herself in an impossible situation.

They said that? They used that term? That I'm a trauma vampire? No, I don't think so. There are always a few bad apples, aren't there? But teaching is more of a *spiritual* calling than anything else. Of course I *cared* about Sarah on a personal level. She is smart and good with even the most difficult kids, and we share the same style sense. We are both the kind of people that if we had chosen to work in another field, advertising or finance, we would be rich.

My husband tells me all the time that he would *kill* for someone like me. He is a cofounder of Tabor Capital—they were one of the first groups to fund Cheksy—and even *he* says it's about relationships. And trust me, Mike isn't what you'd call a warm person. He sees his goal and he goes for it, no matter what. So, if even *he* can see the value in fostering close, personal relationships . . . He's always saying that if he had me on his team, he'd never lose an acquisition. I'd get my man every time.

And I do.

But I *chose* to be here instead. A public servant. And Sarah did too. I consider her my mentee. But the relationship *never* went beyond that.

I'm sorry, I might be a little confused about the time line. Are you asking about Sarah and Crispin? I don't like what you're implying.

I'm a mother for God's sake.

16

Adam

THIS DAY WAS careening farther and farther from the
rails. Maybe he should just call the police. But that
package. Drugs and *poison*? What the hell was the poison about? What had Tina been thinking to include *actual
poison?*

What a stupid idea it had been. Only, he'd *hated* Kemp.
Always around. So smug with his king-maker job, his
charmed life, his easy health, the way he got Ali. He didn't
deserve Ali. Ali was an artist, she was free, she *shouldn't*
have been with Kemp. That tech bro. That life high-
scorer. That man who had the professional ascendency
Adam himself would have charted had things not gone so
wrong. After Kemp began dating Ali, Adam googled him
obsessively. And there, a needle in a haystack, he found a
minor scandal in the froth of news, in *Willamette Week*
or *The Oregonian*. A local businesswoman who owned a
chain of tea shops called The Dips (Had Adam been to
one? He thought he had. The white glow was too bright

for pregnant Sarah. They turned. They fled.) had been the victim of a nefarious prank. Packages of drugs showing up at her place of work from the dark web, addressed to her. Sent, it was accused, by one C. Kemp. The article didn't outright say that Kemp and this business owner were lovers, but it was an easy gap to jump.

Adam googled the shop and found the owner. She looked kind of like Sarah, only with a little more linen, a little more woo-woo, better lighting. A married woman with a young child.

Had he been asked, Adam would have said he felt no particular claim to Ali. She was just the neighbor. So then how did he explain the clenching anger that overtook him when Kemp began holing up in her room? The sense of dread that came over him when that all-black-everything truck pulled up each night, bouncing on its huge, off-road tires that wouldn't so much as taste the dirt their entire life cycle? Maybe it was the sense of territory invaded. Or, his better angel, maybe he wanted to protect Ali from this evil doppelgänger. Maybe he just had good instincts.

And the plan came to him, fully formed, like your child delivered with her personality intact. After all, it wasn't so hard. Kemp had shown him the way. One package was debatable or an anomaly or bad luck. Two was a pattern.

He waited until he saw Tina skate off on her longboard. Then he followed in his car, Maddie strapped into her seat in the back. When they were far enough away, where nobody from the neighborhood would see them, Adam pulled up on her. He made a deal while Maddie babbled behind him. He wanted drugs. He wanted whatever shady shit Tina could get into a box.

"What are you trying to do?" Tina wondered, eyes hooded, suspicious. Probably, if Adam had not lived on the street for years, she would have taken him for an under-cover cop. *Hey there, friend-o, where do the cool kids get the drugs?* Instead, she seemed bemused.

"You and your girl looking to get high?"

"It's just for a . . . look, it doesn't matter, right?"

"I don't want you killing anyone," Tina said.

"I'm not going to kill anyone," Adam said. "I'm not even going to take any of it. Just make it as hardcore as you can. Make it as spooky as possible. It's to prove a point."

"Alright," she said, eyeing Maddie gesturing to the air in her car seat. "But I'm not part of any point you're trying to make, you got that? *Any* of this shit comes back to me, it's *I don't know shit, officer*, and it's also you and little Ms. Stepford getting your lives fucked with, forever and ever, amen."

"Of course," Adam said, making the sign of the cross. "Of course."

Tina overcharged, probably—$500—but Adam didn't care. She delivered a few days later. She left the box in the hedge in front of his house, and Adam didn't even look inside when he retrieved it. He slapped on a printed label with the address of Ali's work on it and a Logicstyx sticker Kemp had given him like a party favor the first time they met. Then he drove out to Vancouver, to the closest mail collection box to Kemp's parents. Maddie watched him from the car. He kept looking around, waiting for a clear scene. No cars. No witnesses. Maybe he shouldn't do this. Would there be cell phone tracking to pin him to this exact location? Were there cameras? These days there were always cameras. There were cameras in people's doorbells for God's sake. He had to do it. He was taking Maddie to a story hour at the Vancouver library after this. Just in case he needed an alibi. The longer he stood there, on the edge of doing it, the more likely he was to get into trouble. He pushed the box in. It rang out against the bottom like the starting bell for some off-kilter race.

That would be it, Adam thought. He'd settled the scales. Ali would report the box of drugs, Kemp would be tied to it, along with his history of recurring behavior, and his life would be fucked up a little. He wasn't a good guy, Adam reminded himself. He wasn't a good guy.

* * *

Adam walked a little faster down the street. Away, away, away. Ali was missing, and he couldn't call the police. If she was really gone, then that box, those drugs, he'd be connected to *all* of it. The police would come snooping around, and Charlie would helpfully inform them that, actually, a drug dealer had been hanging around Adam's house lately. Why had he done it? Oh why? He could have at least been more careful. He could have worn gloves. But he wasn't sleeping enough. Maddie was always in his ear. Babies always *needed*. He hadn't been *careful* in months, hadn't been capable of being careful, and now he was connected.

Something Candice said spiked in his mind. Ali's Internet diary. Adam stopped in his tracks. Perhaps there was some kind of clue there. It was easy to find her. The blogger platform was all but abandoned as a product, Spartan and bare-bones. Searching her email address led him to the account. He read too hungrily, ingesting the posts whole, and his mind felt sickened. Mr. Handsome. Window Boo. Something had happened, and it was Kemp. It was him. She was definitely getting worried in the posts, but there was something else there too.

Kemp always going to her window. Always looking out. Why was he always looking out?

When Sarah had come up on him holding the shingle, he was still wind-knocked, a piece of Ali's roof in hand. He had been on the edge of realizing something. Then she talked to him, she hugged him, but he had begun to know, he realized, even then he *knew* something. In her voice, in her desperate cling to him. He had been standing in the exact spot that Kemp had the night before. Holding his dick, staring back at the house. Only now Adam realized that he never had to worry about Kemp seeing him and Maddie in the window, because Kemp hadn't been looking. From that spot, in that moment, Adam had seen what Kemp had seen the night before. It was their bedroom. It was Sarah.

CHAPTER

17

Kemp

EIGHT DARK DAYS since Sarah had cut things off and
Crispin was bereft. Time passed, didn't it? The date on
his phone dutifully changed, the weather trended darker
and wetter, but this pain hurt in a way that seemed like it
would never cease, like a lost limb. He got out of bed and
into the shower, a long, scalding session that reddened his
shoulders where the spray hit. Knob turned all the way,
though he wished it would go hotter. More, more, more.
Boil and render him, send him down the drain with the
scummy water. Soap bubbling in the dish. He kept washing himself, the bar of white, jasmine-scented soap getting
smaller. A sea slug. Dissolving. His skin itched. He wasn't
here enough. Echoey absence of life. Too many nights at his
parents' place. What did this make him? This house looked
like it was inhabited by a squatter.

He frothed up his hands and jerked off furiously until
some of the soap got into his meatus (what a fucking on-the-
nose name) and burned. Until his penis literally squeaked.

Until he expelled gloomily and sat on the shower floor, waiting for the hot water to run out. It never would. He'd paid extra for on-demand.

He dried, dressed, went out to his car. He was floaty, dehydrated. Pain at the base of his neck. He drove aimlessly, phone faceup on the seat beside him. He felt like he was in a TV show, but which one? He didn't watch much TV. Even when he did, he wasn't actually watching TV.

Crispin turned at random while he drove. This was his neighborhood as much as Sarah's, and yet he was relegated to the shadows.

Was it ideal to be sleeping with a teacher at his mom's school? No, it was not ideal. But the heart, a tangled bastard, wanted what it wanted. He had been his mom's little pet for so long, there were probably connections he wasn't seeing. Underpinning psychological needs this affair scratched. Who knew. He just considered it incredibly compelling to love someone *despite* all that was positioned against them.

Since the night Sarah undressed for him at his mother's party, giving him that command to come on something that was *theirs*, she had been a super element that gave him superpowers, and now she wanted him to go back to being a mortal. They'd only been together for two weeks, give or take. It wasn't enough. It wasn't nearly enough. He deserved more. He deserved it all.

He passed a martial arts studio, a National Park themed bar, the New Seasons on 41st. This was where he would turn to get to her house. A great victory to continue straight ahead, trembling until he got to the light at César Chávez, the bustle and glare of Hawthorne proper before him.

When Sarah told him that they should stop seeing each other, he didn't believe her. He saw her out and they even kissed goodbye. So this couldn't be the end-end. End-ends, as he well knew, came with dramatics, big tears, actions you regretted later. They didn't happen while you were looking for an earring, wondering where the keys were, and asking *Would you like a tea?* A light kiss on dry lips.

But it had been eight days, and no word from her.

He should just drive home, fire up Tinder or OkCupid or Hinge, and get *over her*. He couldn't bear to. He refused. Besides, which "home" would he go to? To his mother and father's mansion, where they drifted past each other in silence? Or to the shell on 50th, empty, empty, empty but for the cabinets stacked to bursting with tea. So much tea. He wondered, turning left onto Chávez, if there was a place that would take a bulk donation of high-end tea. Or maybe he'd sell it on Craigslist to some enterprising tea shop owner. Maybe he would dump it all in a hot bath and soak himself.

He'd bought the tea for Tamara, the woman he'd loved before Sarah. She owned a tea shop. Tea shops. One, two, seven. An expanding empire of white spaces clad in living walls of succulents, fragrant, idling whiffs of far-off places, stationed by a continuous stream of people working on their laptops, buying $5 cookies, sniffing samples as if they knew what they were doing. But nobody knew what they were doing. They just liked the ritual, the spectacle, the show that assured them *this* was worth it.

But Crispin knew the secret of the world: hardly anything was worth it.

Tamara *loved* the tea. He knew she would. He was that kind of lover. She opened each cabinet like it was a treasure chest. She called out the varietals and the points of origin of each tea with an increasing ardor. He really had spared no expense. Then Tamara walked through the living room, the bare walls, the open doors. He'd been thrilled at the echoing clatter their steps made in the empty space, as though there were more people walking with them. Little feet. The little feet of the life he would one day have with her.

"Houses aren't supposed to be empty," he told Tamara, as they climbed the stairs.

"No," she said from behind him. "They aren't." The maybe, if, and when. He was happy. Because in the days after he'd closed the deal, gotten the keys, waiting to show her, the place felt loose, overbig, and unwieldy. What had he done? Buying a house to impress a woman? What was wrong with him? He needed her in here as soon as possible.

"Well, it's not all the way empty," he said, opening the door to the main bedroom and wincing. The effect hadn't come off. The mattress lay like a murder victim in the center of the empty bedroom. It had nothing of the spare romance he'd intended. But she didn't seem to care or even notice.

"It's perfect," Tamara said.

That was the week she met his family. A dinner at the house. How his mother loved her. His father even seemed to deviate from his normal rote programming, asking about the tea shops and marveling at how deftly she'd scaled up. He liked her because he saw her as a valuable asset. And she liked the game too, showing off her plan to open shops in Seattle and San Francisco, maybe even LA. She asked him for advice, and the old man ruffled his feathers and gave it. She called him Mike. She teased him. She complimented his mother on her dress, her drapes, her countertops. Crispin beamed. He was so proud. Tamara was going to divorce her husband, move into his townhome, and fill it with all the things he didn't know how to buy.

"Look at this view," his mother said as they stepped onto the balcony. "Not a neighbor for miles, but we have Portland, right there, just for us."

Tamara looked at the glittering lights, and Crispin looked at her. He would give her anything she wanted. It was perfect.

Until it wasn't. They used to get high on his top deck and ask each other what time it was and marvel at how little of it had passed.

A lot of it had passed now.

Last he'd heard, she'd gotten involved in an investigation of some kind after a large package of knockoff oxycontin showed up at her office. What a shocker. Of all people. You just never knew.

What a shame.

But it served her right. She had complicated his life with her lies. She had told him that she loved him. Only he'd been sloppy when he mailed the package. There'd somehow been *something* to point back at him, and he never learned what exactly. Footage of him dropping the package in the blue mailbox on Glisan? It obviously wasn't good to have court actions on the record. She tried to get a restraining order, and the case was briefly noted in the *Willamette Week*. Which meant his fucking name was out there for anyone to see. And all because of a harmless prank.

CHAPTER

18

Sarah

SARAH PACED THE living room, watching Adam on his phone outside, slinking off with his call. She was agitated and passed this off to Maddie, in her arms. Hot, cranky baby, not having any of it. She pulled at Sarah's blouse. She wanted in; she wanted to nurse. What had Adam said? *Go take her off the shelf. Go actually play with her. Go feed her.* Go feed her? Adam *knew* how hard it was for her to produce milk. That he would poke her *there?* Maddie screamed and kicked her legs harder.

"I can't, Maddie!" she yelled. "I don't have anything in me."

Her baby stopped fussing, looked up at her with red, wet cheeks, then wailed all the louder. Sarah pulled her in closer, stepped with her, rocking.

"I'm so sorry, I'm so sorry," she said.

He had let Maddy sleep. Why had Adam let her go to sleep? It had all gone wrong. She had seen him staring at the shingle, *still* obsessed with that girl Ali. And the way that he looked at her. Did he know about her and Kemp? Did he? Did he know it all? Is that why he'd been so cruel? Did he know last night, the night before, back when it first started? When had he first figured it out? Sarah shivered. She was tired. Her life was blurring. Nightmare and reality. Was there anything left for them, when all the secrets came free? If she ever told him about Kemp, about what had started as innocuous payback but had degenerated and twisted into some kind of trap she couldn't break free of, would they really stand a chance?

She was just so tired.

She had meant to come home and make him understand: *I love you.* She had meant for him to know: *You work so hard to keep this family going, and I want you to know that I see that. I want you to know that I know I haven't been the easiest person to live with. I want you to know that I recognize being a stay-at-home dad, all the messages society tells you, I know it's hard, but you're doing so great.*

She wanted to say, *All my girlfriends are jealous of me because of what you do for this family.*

Kemp had fucked it all up. The fact that he'd left his truck parked outside the house. What he'd pulled last night, dick in hand. He was sabotaging everything. He *wanted* it out in the open because what did he have to lose? She hadn't said the things she wanted to. She couldn't make Adam understand that she loved him, that she loved him so much. If he knew about Kemp, then he needed to know that it was her way of keeping them together. After Ali . . . They say two wrongs don't make a right, but whoever *they* were had obviously never been married. It was basic math. Being with Crispin had made her value Adam.

For a moment, she'd seen a path emerge in the fog that had descended upon their marriage. A path that would lead them away from Ali and Kemp, and back to themselves. Back to that boy she had met at a party in college on any old night that had turned into this, her whole life.

Finally, Maddie fell back asleep. A dribble of milk navigated the crevasses of her many chins, her Nero neck. Her mouth popped off the nipple and Sarah began to cry. Tears that seemed to be of one, long piece, ferrying out a load of bile-like emotion. What had she been thinking with Crispin? She had let it go too far. She had done so many things wrong.

The fog closed in. She was alone, on a mountain, with no way back to her marriage. They would not make it. Crispin had been right. She and Adam would continue to grow apart, they would divorce, and he would be a could-have-been she had to see whenever they traded Maddie between their barren, miserly lives.

Sarah leaned back and closed her eyes. A vertiginous space opened up beneath her heart, and it was all she could do to catch her breath. She loved him. She didn't want to fail at this. She wasn't used to failing. She was breathing so hard she would wake Maddie up again. Her phone buzzed. A randomized number she didn't know but knew all too well. Kemp had long ago figured out some way to send her texts through a cloud-based service that blah-blah-blah and spat out his messages from randomized numbers that would look like spam if Adam ever found one. No two ever the same. It was the perfect system except for the delay. Sometimes his texts would arrive late by minutes or even hours. Her heart chilled. His truck was still out there on the street. He was still in her life.

Don't go, the text read. I don't know what I'll be forced to do if you leave me.

Sarah looked at Maddie with melting, love-wobbled eyes. Her baby. Her sweet, forever baby. She felt a rush of endorphins. This was worth it. This was worth everything. She would fight. Because, otherwise, Kemp wouldn't stop. He wasn't going to let Sarah go. No matter what, he wouldn't give up. Even right then, he was probably somewhere in *that* house; he was probably watching her.

Well, she thought, *watch this*.

She strapped Maddie into the BabyBjörn carrier. Her baby gurgled sleepily but stayed in a fitful slumber. She smacked her lips, a warm lump of love. Act quickly, now. Adam could be back at any moment. Sarah left the house, nose in the sparse hair at Maddie's scalp. She crossed the street. She knew the code to the 4Runner and where Kemp kept a key in the center console. Fast. She had to be fast. *Fuck Kemp*, she kept thinking to herself. *Fuck Kemp*.

She started the car, not bothering to buckle the seat belt and risk waking Maddie where she lay strapped to her chest. She drove up Salmon Street. The cab smelled like him. Woodsy spice. She rolled down all the windows.

Would he be mad? He would be *furious*.

CHAPTER

19

Adam

ADAM WANTED TO cry. He had made it all the way to Main and César Chávez. But it was his feet moving, his body passing through space. Inside, he was numb. Events passed him like he was the background in a stage play. Kemp had been looking at Sarah. And now Ali was missing. The two things seemed connected, but how could they add up? Across the boulevard, Fred Meyers squatted, huge and humming with shoppers getting midweek groceries. Traffic whooshed by, the homeless (houseless?) gathered around the bottle deposit, shuffling along their rattly carts. Two squirrels faced off on the trunk of a tree, little claws scritching as one tried to get around the other. Adam felt pressure in his forehead, building down to the base of his nose. It was a bright, crisp fall day. Everything seemed normal.

Uneasy, intrusive thoughts about what he had begun to realize paraded through his head. Sarah and Crispin. His wife. That . . . that man. The daylight fading. Fall and then winter. It was inevitable. Soon it would be dark by now. Soon there would be only rain. The traffic light on Main changed, and a pod of bikers pedaled past. People with their pants cinched tight on one ankle to stay clear of the chain, helmets atop serious, tired faces. The flaps of a blouse or dress shirt peeking free under the bottom of their tropical bright raincoats. These were the professionals, covering the final tired blocks on their way home. Not too long ago, he had been among them, probably with a podcast in his ear, something about the NBA or the most recent idiocy of whatever congressman doing whatever horrible thing, or, if he was feeling self-improvey, something on science or history. Riding in line with others like him, flashing lights, gloved hands, sweat dripping away the stress of another day at work.

But Sarah and Kemp. Kemp and Sarah. Ali. The shingle.

Maybe he deserved it. This sinking hole in his chest. The sense that the world was laughing at him. *Shame, shame, shame.* They kept hurting each other. Maybe a marriage was only a measure of how much hurt you could withstand and then carry on.

Adam remembered the last time he'd been like these people. But it had been the middle of the day, and bright June too. How empty the streets were, summer-hot riding, his backpack bulging with all the things from his desk. Something, the corner of a picture frame maybe, poked into his back. Maddie in the hospital with the little purple knit cap they gave all newborns, made by volunteers, to remind new parents that when a baby cried uncontrollably, it was normal. Don't shake the baby. It's normal. Where did all those purple caps go? Among the drifts of castoffs in a Goodwill warehouse? The things that hold meaning won't always. Of course you wouldn't shake a baby. Of course violence was never the answer. In the photo, he and Sarah are beaming and tired. Happy, but worn thin. It sat stuffed inside his bag with fidget balls and coffee mugs on the day he'd been fired.

The conference room was cold, air-conditioning too high. It wasn't even lunch. He remembered that because when he left his job forever, he left his Tupperware of fried rice in the mini fridge. Their best Tupperware. The one that never leaked and didn't allow lingering smells or flavors. Why did he know that? Would anyone with a real life know that? Would his best friends from college, Liam or Jamie, know *that* about Tupperware? No, his friends were real people with real jobs and real concerns. Adam endeavored to not care. But when Kelly emailed him to ask if he wanted him to mail it to his house, Adam dutifully responded with his address.

"It's regrettable," his boss said, sitting across the table, a cross-section of a massive tree, the live edges maintained, splayed open to the very heart of it. He was an erect, oddly formal man, originally from some Scandinavian country, Denmark or Norway. Adam could never remember which one, because, as the man liked to tell, he'd moved between the two frequently growing up but hated one and loved the other. "Because I do appreciate the work you have done for us here at Lostine Windows." He had founded the company when he was in Oregon on a study abroad. Hiking in the Wallowa Mountains, out along the Lostine River, an inspiration about glass taken from the clarity of that water. Thirty years later, here he was, firing Adam. In some ways, he was always meant to fire Adam, even back then as a young man with his feet in icy waters, spying on the bottom-feeding life of crawdads. We are, all of us, seeds for every terrible or wonderful thing we will do.

"I—" but Adam stopped. He couldn't talk. Regrettably it was because he might cry. His nose ticked with the heat of tears. Which, considering the circumstances, was too pathetic to bear. Surely it should take more than this? He hadn't even particularly liked this job. He certainly gave no shits about glass.

"You don't have to say anything," his boss said. "But you do realize we cannot have that here at Lostine Windows. There is a standard of decency and safety we must abide by. And that kind of behavior, even if I could overlook it, would hold too much potential for litigation. It is clearly stated in the employee manual."

Adam nodded. A big part of his job had been posting drooly photos of luxury houses high in the hills of some city or another showcasing Lostine windows. The clarity of the glass was supposedly much better than any other on the market. Some kind of alchemy, proprietary and spoken of with great reverence by the boss, allowed you to see clearer. Their slogan, thought up by Adam and tinkered to death by his boss until it felt lifeless and alien, was *See a better future with TruView windows by Lostine.* Too wordy, but it was on *everything*, all of their marketing material, and Adam couldn't help but feel a little proud.

That morning, while his boss and most of the production crew had an intense meeting about a recent shipment that arrived at a hotel site in Hawaii with half the panes cracked, Adam was supposed to be scheduling just such posts. Which he did, for a time, before growing bored with the over-the-top hashtagging of houses as #heavenhome or #lifegoals or whatever. He toggled over to his personal Instagram account, taking advantage of the empty office. There was a photo of a woman on the search page who looked *just* like Ali. She was doing a little dance, smiling, clapping along to the lyrics. Young and bright, her whole future ahead of her. Had he ever had that? He missed that. Before baby and wife and home remodel. Her smile seemed to say, we both know this is ridiculous, but . . .

The Internet gods knew him. More often, it seemed, the women on his feed looked like Ali, that woman across the street he'd found himself thinking of more and more. Was the algorithm answering his appetite or whetting it? Either way, he clicked on the photo and still couldn't be sure that it wasn't *actually* her. His neighbor. It was just for curiosity's sake. But that wasn't true. Why had he done it on his computer? His life might have been saved, *none of this* might have happened, if he'd just been like any normal person and taken his phone to the toilet and sat, balls turning cold over the water, and pawed the screen there.

But he'd been done in by his own squirrely over-thinking. To get to the bathroom, you had to pass by the conference room. He would be seen by the people in the meeting. His bathroom visit would be timed, in a way, by all in attendance. No, he was here, in the office, alone for at least another half hour, and at Lostine Windows, meetings always went long due to didactic monologues by the boss. So he checked behind him. And again. And if you had to check twice, you checked once more. He even did a loop around the office. Double, double, double sure. But it wasn't enough. Or maybe he'd been so drawn in that he hadn't noticed something he should have. The stutter of a chair being pushed away. The muffled slide of a door running along smooth rails. And maybe the woman in the photo didn't look all that much like Ali really. Maybe he was just lamenting his lost youth. Pathetic, early-onset midlife crisis. But it didn't matter, did it? It was a one-way window. Nobody knew he was staring. Here was soft lighting, bulging cleavage, a giggly face. Come with me, it seemed to say, come. Before he knew exactly what had happened, he was on the woman's personal site, pictures of her naked body from every imaginable angle, growing hard beneath his desk. The cool, cement building, the exposed cement office, the brushed steel and acres of TruView glass. He always felt a perpetual chill here. But this warmed him. Sarah hadn't touched him in months, and that wasn't an excuse, but also, Adam didn't feel like himself and hadn't in a long while. Here was a physical lever he could pull, an animal before-and-after effect.

He didn't know how long his boss had been watching, or if he caught on that Adam's hand was working under his desk. It was too long. He became aware of his boss's presence by the repeated clearing of his black-scarved, Scandinavian throat.

"I understand," Adam managed to say.

"Good," the boss said. "You can clear your things today, or I can meet you here, this weekend, if you need more time and would rather do it in privacy. I won't tell the team any of the details. I'll say it was a mutual decision. I'll even say you've had another opportunity that was too good to pass up, if you'd like."

Adam wanted to do it right away. He never wanted to see his boss or the office again. He packed up his desk as quickly as he could, everyone watching from the bunkers of their work stations, returning cautiously from the meeting,

the news spreading by some convection he couldn't understand. Google chat? Twitter? Nobody seemed to be talking, but he was sure it had gotten out. Here walks the
pervert. Stand clear.

He rode his bike home and found Sarah and Maddie
in the front yard in the soft June sun, lying on a blanket
side by side and looking up at the thick green leaves that
shaded their house each summer. She was fresh into her
summer break and Maddie was a shiny miracle. Adam
wished he'd stopped at a bar and gotten soaked instead of
coming home and being presented with all he had thrown
away.

"What a nice surprise!" Sarah said.

"It's . . . I—" and he told her almost everything, right
then. He couldn't help it. They were still like that then,
he thought. No secrets. She was perfect, even caught up
in the beginnings of what he would come to recognize as
depression, she was everything, and he'd betrayed that. He
was a puddle, a ribbon of oil in a puddle, the dirty gravel
speck at the bottom of an oil-ridden puddle on a pot-holed
stretch of industrial road. The only thing to do was to lay
himself bare. Seek forgiveness through supplication.

"Well, that's bullshit," Sarah said when he finished,
shocking him into feeling the sun on his arms, the chatter
of birds in the air. "You'll find another."

"Another what?"

"Another job, Adam."

She allowed him to turn away from his embarrassment
and find anger instead. She was right. He didn't deserve
this! He had done so much good work for them, made
them so much money! He wrote their goddamn slogan!
This pivot from shame fueled his search for another job.

All through the summer. But it seemed as though the incident followed him. In some of the small hours, he even wondered if his boss had quietly circulated the circumstances of his termination to every other employer in Portland. A secret society. Stay back! Beware! Here walks the pervert.

When fall came into sight, when Sarah was preparing to go back to work, they just sort of shifted into him being a SAHD. They even began to reframe it to their family and friends as a sanctimonious choice. *We just couldn't* stand *the thought of Maddie with strangers. She's so young! There will never be another time when one of us can do this!*

Are you sure it's Biblical? her mother had asked them.

And Sarah, preeminent badass, said, *Who cares?* She held Adam's hand, filling him to the top. *It's the best thing he could ever do for our family.*

And for most of the summer, he really believed that too. They were home together. They were only about Maddie. They were happy. They were so happy, weren't they?

But as Sarah ramped up to go back to work, she shifted away from him, from them, and began obsessing over the incoming year she hadn't thought she would be bothering with. Maternity leave. Instead she had to be made permanent. For their family. For the remodel. For everything. Things started to become too much. She began to wander through the most overgrown path in the forest of her postpartum funk. He fell again. Thinking about Ali. He could almost see into her window, but for the trees. Then a fast, cranky storm managed that for him. It felt like fate. A felled branch almost crushed their Subaru Outback and brought her window into view. Was he looking to re-create the terms of his termination? Who knew? Ali's window wasn't an image on Instagram's search page. It was right across the street. It was broadcast only for him, each night never to be repeated.

So look what happened to him then. One thing and another, always following each other. *What did he do, did he . . .*

"Fuck!" Adam said. Some of the bikers shushing past, tires slick in fall muck, looked at him. He knew what they were thinking. He would have thought the same. Look at that insane man in his stained sweats, his unwashed hair, his dirty mouth. He probably "day trades." He probably "used to look good in college." He's probably "very good at fantasy basketball" and "has a tip about a new crypto currency."

It was worse than that. He was a peeper, a pervert, a cuckold. A poison-buyer, a distracted father, a failure.

When was the last time Adam worked out? He should be eating better, reading more, meditating at least once a day. He used to love the rock gym. He used to have a climbing crew. He was a SAHD! He had so much time! And he was wasting it. Of course Sarah had needed some-one else.

What had he done? What horrible, disgusting things had he done? He should get some help. He felt grossed out by his own body. He smelled bad, his fingernails were too long. He needed to shave and cut his hair. He cringed, a shrug, a shiver, as if he could shed his own body and be free of his jumbled, dark wants, leaving them behind like molted snakeskin.

Adam began walking home. There was, after all, no other place to go. He had a bitter thought: Was it his fault that Sarah cheated on him? Had he been enough? And even worse, had he, somehow, gotten Ali entangled in this? Was he the reason she'd gone missing?

Their . . . dates in the window. He'd been promising something he hadn't realized. He was her emergency contact for God's sake. That last post on her Instagram, the shadow man in the window, that "art," it *was* him. Watching over her and haloed in light. But he hadn't watched over her. He'd only taken, taken, taken. Taken advantage of what she offered through glass. And when he was done, he shut her out again without a thought, as if that thin membrane absolved him from the consequences. He'd been suspicious of Kemp. God, for how long had he been suspicious? And what had he done? Fuck all.

Kemp had taken Ali. Kemp had taken Sarah. It was up to him to make sure Kemp would take no more.

He rounded back onto Salmon Street, rain beginning to fall, someone's tin-shed roof calling out. It was almost dark, but there was a trick Adam didn't quite catch. Something missing on this stretch he'd walked, biked, driven hundreds of times, memorized in ways deeper than thinking, as you do with anything you live with. And then he had it: Kemp's 4Runner was gone. He had already gotten away.

20

Kemp

S UDDENLY, CRISPIN WAS starving. But he wouldn't go
back to that house. It wasn't a house at all, or at least not
his. Not without Sarah. He just owned it. It was a model of
a life he'd been interested in—can you tell me more about
the features?—but had realized wasn't, actually, for him at
all. Sarah hated that house. She hated *all* the new construction rushed up and down the big SE streets—Foster, Pow-
ell, Division, Hawthorne, Belmont—and lusted instead
over the ancient farmhouses and craftsmen that were saggy,
and blocky, and porch-ridden. The ones that needed endless work and leaked and sparked and creaked. What she
wanted was what she had. An old house, renovated to feel
new. He'd call his real estate agent tomorrow and tell her
he wanted to sell. He'd probably make a ton of money too.

He went through the drive-through at SuperDeluxe
and over-ordered. But he was ravenous, so who cared? How
much tea had he drank in the last few days? An uninten-
tional cleanse. He would muddy his insides anew.

At the next window, he picked up two hamburgers, a small white bag of fried chicken pieces, and a shallow, sweated-through paper bag of french fries. The girl at the window had a nose ring.

"I like that," he said. "The ring."

"Shit, yeah," she said, handing over his Coke. "My boyfriend hates it."

Her boyfriend. Brought up so quickly. A message. *Lay off.* When had it become assumed that any kind of conversation was a pickup line? It was shallow-hearted. It was the modern world. He ate as he drove, and the grease in his mouth, hot and salty, was so good that it was sexual. An expansion into the world. Over the smaller things. Crush the fowl and bovine meat between thy teeth.

We all used to be a part of a tribe, he thought. *Out in the world, taking what we needed.*

It's only foolish if it doesn't work out.

I can't let that happen.

Crispin wasn't hungry any longer. He dropped the food out his window at the next light. Two guys sitting at North Bar, cigarettes fireflying around pint glasses, watched him.

"Hey, man, that's messed up," one of them said. "There's hungry people out here."

"*I'm* hungry," the other one said, and laughed.

"Then pick it up," Crispin said. "Fucking crawl over here like a little bitch dog and pick up that trash food with your goddamn mouth."

Then he rolled up the window and squealed off on green, leaving their stunned, do-nothing faces behind. He'd given up too easy with Tamara, and now she was pregnant again with that loser husband. He wouldn't make that mistake a second time. Sarah wouldn't get away. She deserved that. He was saving her. She would come to understand. He drove straight to her forbidden street. This was the first time he was seeing her house in person. On Google Street View, the house that showed up was the old place: flaking white paint; sagging, moss-riddled roof; sloping porch. Now, the place looked like it had drunk from the fountain of youth. It seemed to sit up straighter, fresh paint snapping its lines. Red with a white picket fence. Sarah called it her dream house.

Crispin laughed out loud. Her dream. It was so small, in the end. It was nothing. He could afford something twice as much as this, three times, and closer in, or farther out, whatever she wanted. He was looking so intently at the house that he didn't see the woman getting out of her car. He almost ran her over.

"Open your eyes!" she shouted at him.

A woman was yelling at him—was she drunk?— and he slammed on the brakes as she flipped him off; he watched her walk up the steps and disappear into the run-down house just across the street from Sarah's.

After a short while, a light went on in the upstairs bedroom. It was a Thursday. Soon he would learn about Thursday 2000s nights at The Turtle. Soon he would learn that her name was Ali. Soon he would see that her window was the one that looked into all he wanted to have and to hold and to never let go.

His love would never embarrass him again. This time, he would be smart, decisive, and he would take action. This time, he had found a way to stay close enough to change her mind.

21

Sarah

S HE NEVER MEANT to sleep with Crispin. Well, obviously, in the actual moment, the *moments*, yes, that was
her intention. He didn't *take* her. If anything, at least in
the beginning, it was Sarah who took him. Led him up
to the reading room in Evie Kemp's house, put on a show.
How *powerful* she'd felt. Telling him what to do. So it kept
going. Cedar smell, bright and clear, flannel shirts made
of a thicker fabric, of some higher quality than she and
Adam could afford. She gripped, pulled, tried to destroy,
and Kemp would smile and laugh, teeth out, body ready.

She never meant for it to go so far.

Even if she had set out to cheat on Adam, settle the
score in her heart, there were smarter ways. Find someone
wholly unconnected with her world. Anonymous trysts in
airport hotel rooms with careworn carpets and taut bed-
spreads. It was probably easy enough. There were entire
platforms engineered to bring just such people together. So

why the son of the school's principal? If she had to cheat on her husband, why not with *anyone* else?

When she first saw him at that party in Evie's house, those strange, periodic flexes of her boss to show what money could buy, Sarah didn't know he was her son. This was the absolute truth. He looked *nothing* like her. Nothing! The initial spark with Crispin wasn't because he was a Kemp. She couldn't bear to think that she'd sought him out and entangled herself in some kind of Freudian struggle. That fucking Crispin felt like fucking over Evie too. That perhaps Evie's suggestive texts *hadn't* been something she'd wholly laughed off. That maybe she'd just found another way in. Sick girl that she was.

No, nothing like that.

You're sick!

No, absolutely not.

At the first party, Evie's birthday, Adam was being, well, himself. He wanted to go home early. He made fun of everything he saw, a little desperate and grasping, as if in mocking it all he might be inoculated from jealousy. Which, of course, was useless. They were all a little jealous. Big, granite countertops; wide, airy space; brass chandeliers that looked like some turn-of-the-century experiment, birthing Edison bulbs at the terminus of each spindly ray.

And that view.

It had always been considered witty to mock Vancouver. It was viewed as Portland's little cousin just over the river in Washington, referred to simply as the Armpit, or the Couv. It was a place people used to slum for cheap nights out and the high-in-the-sky fireworks that were illegal in Oregon. But Evie's house was miles east of the Armpit, almost to Government Island. From her balcony, it seemed as if Portland were performing for them, twinkling and dancing in the hazy distance. And Sarah, despite not wanting to, could understand the appeal. Up here in the hills, clean and spacious, with a river view, the city glowed their way. It was a complete change in register from Portland, from Chávez Elementary, where the church across the street attracted a large houseless population, where she routinely saw smashed needles on her way to work, where she'd once found two arrows ominously buried deeply in the flesh of the Seussian curly willow that grew in the center of the field. It was incredible that Evie Kemp moved from this world to that and back again like a minor god alighting each day onto a dirty world. She had the work, she had the wealth, she had *everything*.

Sarah knew Evie's husband was some kind of big-deal tech investor in the same way she knew there was a wizard behind the curtain at the end of Dorothy's journey on the Yellow Brick Road. He was the key to everything, but he was invisible. The well-reported rumor out there was that his group was an early funder of Logicstyx, a company which, even Sarah knew from the articles in *Willamette Week* and the *New York Times* as well as from NPR and the chatter among the parents in her classroom, was a surefire fortune-minter. A billionaire factory. Sarah had heard teachers at Chávez Elementary speculate that when Logicstyx went public, Evie and her family would rocket into the generational, found-some-nonprofits, build-a-library, choose-the-next-governor strata of wealth.

Yet, walking around Evie's house, Sarah couldn't see how their life could get more opulent. What else could more money even buy?

"Do you think if we search long enough we can find the magic lamp?" Adam wondered, trying to be funny. Why was he always trying to be funny? He wasn't funny. Had he ever been funny? Sarah remembered laughing, but why? "You think this took all three wishes?"

"Shut up," Sarah said.

"Yikes," Adam said. "OK."

That was mean, but here they were, without Maddie, at a party with free booze and good music, and all he could do was make lame jokes. Ask if she was ready to go home. Sarah kept thinking, *Hey, fuck you, you're missing your big chance. Get your wife a little drunk, maybe we could finally mess around.* Because since Maddie, that had been the last thing Sarah wanted, and the only thing, it seemed, Adam thought about. It felt to Sarah that her body was a scant resource fought over by the locals. To be touched. Everyone in her house wanted to lay claim to her. Adam each night in the bedroom. Maddie all hours of the day and night. Sucking, yearning, pumping, touching. Her world felt rinded in wax gone brittle, flame absent for too long. She picked at the lack of feeling inside her, curious. What's that? What's there? What's under this? She was either numb, dragging through a slosh of cold puddle water, or overloaded with emotion, a jagged prick at the end of a scream. Sarah had the thought seize her just the other day, while walking Maddie around the neighborhood, that her baby's tiny body was the perfect size to fit into the hole of a standard city trash can. She wouldn't even have to take the lid off.

So it felt good—amazing—to be out without the baby, around adult people with adult things to say. She just found herself wishing it wasn't with Adam.

"At the very least, pay attention," Sarah hissed at him. "This house has a lot of fucking glass, doesn't it? Go sell some windows. Help them *see a better future*."

He looked hurt to have the stupid slogan he'd spent months tinkering with quoted back to him. The idea that *that* was his career. She could laugh. Word choice was his greatest professional concern. *Get in the classroom, buddy, report some parents to CPS, try and separate two brawling third-graders, talk down a child with suicidal thoughts, then we can talk.*

In any case, off he went, muttering, slipping along in his poor-me trudge.

And that was when Sarah noticed the man behind the drinks counter. Young and handsome. Beautiful eyes. Blue, bruised color. Big hands. Big, articulate hands. He was staring at Sarah. He was very good about it, only doing it when he thought she couldn't see him, but she could, and she almost lost interest. People were always staring at her. Maddie was a month and a half old, Sarah had lost most of the baby weight, but her tits were still huge. The other day, hot and sweating, each breast veiny and rock-hard with the milk it was dying to let down, nipples screaming against even the slightest wisp of fabric, she walked through the house to get Maddie in only a slip. Adam's eyes almost dropped from his skull. Long cartoon tongue. He told her she looked like a pirate wench. In the best way, he insisted.

There is no best way, she told him. *I don't want to be called a pirate wench.*

Well, you're driving me crazy.

How do you think I feel?

But unlike Adam, this man seemed to sense she was becoming bored with him and so let himself be caught looking. Sarah met his gaze and found she liked to be assessed by these eyes. His manner was white-knuckled, not Sarah's type, but interesting nonetheless.

Of course Sarah asked around about him later, and Ashley told her who he was. Crispin Kemp, her boss's son. And… she found she didn't care. He was a round in the chamber she could choose to use or not.

At the end of that summer, when it turned out Sarah would be going back to work after all, with Adam fired for looking at porn at work and then, Sarah discovered, starting a little game with Ali, Evie held a back-to-school party. Of course, Sarah went alone. She had fallen. How far, how fast. Ali naked and staring back. Everything changed. What Sarah remembered the most was how Ali's body seemed to take up so *much* of Adam. Before Ali vanished into a swirl of curtains, Sarah saw the connection between them. An intense force. And even though Sarah believed him when he insisted nothing physical had ever happened, she didn't care. Which Adam couldn't grasp. He got that she was angry, but *this* angry? He couldn't understand that it might have been better if he had just gone ahead and fucked around with Ali, just so long as they weren't looking at each other *like that*.

There was also the betrayal of difference. Had Ali looked similar to Sarah—small, bird-boned, delicate— would she have been less wounded? If she had also been a type-A, a go-getter, a few years older, would it have hurt less? If, because she wouldn't let him near her, Adam had sought out a facsimile, would she have been cut less deeply? But Ali's image in the glass, big, undeniably beautiful, taking almost all of it up, Californian sun, was something Sarah could never be. It was impossible. For everything that she had, for everything that she was, she would never be that woman in the window.

Most marriages, Sarah knew, went through hard years. Hell, this was America. Almost half didn't even make it. But before she'd caught him, Sarah had understood their troubles as a side effect of a distancing that was universal. A mutual curling inward. Each their own. *They* weren't connected with each other because they weren't connected with *anyone* aside from Maddie. But here Adam was, obviously enraptured by this woman. *Connecting* with her, one window to another, through glass.

"Show me something," Sarah said to Kemp at that second party. "Show me something in this house people don't usually get to see."

Now, Sarah found herself reliving that moment of undressing before him as she drove his truck up into the lap of Mount Tabor with Maddie strapped to her chest. She wished she could stop her memory right there. End it with the striptease. That was the best it ever was with Crispin. A perfect condition: to have taken revenge but also to maintain high ground. What did she have now? She was stealing a car. She was driving with her baby strapped to her chest, no seatbelt. She was reckless.

Still, when she parked the car illegally at the side of the upper loop of Tabor, when she got out and threw the keys over the ledge with all of Portland supplicating at her feet, she felt triumphant. The car would be towed, or vandalized, or stolen.

"You are my sunshine, my only sunshine" she sang to Maddie as she began her long walk home. Adam had almost poisoned that well long ago. Who could have known how sad that song was? Now, she didn't care. Now, she would only sing the parts she liked.

22

Adam

A DAM WAS ALONE in the kitchen. Adam had thoughts. Adam was harried by thoughts when he was alone in the kitchen. Or alone anywhere. Intrusive Thought Radio, all the hits, turned up to ten! Kemp's rig was gone. But Ali was in danger, maybe dead. Where was Ali? What had Candice said? That Kemp had been "coming around"? Looking into Adam's bedroom window. Had Sarah been looking back out? The circumstances of his life. Mosquitos sensing blood. A single, big-bootied ant charged up the side of the range hood. Alone. With purpose. Too late in the season by far. Go home, little ant. Soon it will be winter. You could never get rid of ants.

"Hey, Siri," Adam said. "Call Liam."

He needed to talk to *someone*. Liam lived on the Oregon Coast. He owned waders and a fly-tying station. He'd built his own deck and it was beautiful. He was a biologist, helping salmon recover in a series of rivers and streams that had been muddled and impeded by pollution and dams.

Liam was married. Almost everyone Adam knew was married. But Liam and his husband enjoyed a peaceful life of distinct interests with occasional, pleasant alignment. It seemed like Liam had actually done what so many wedding vows claimed: married his best friend.

Liam didn't answer.

"Hey, this is Liam, leave a—"

Adam hung up. There was a note—*taking Maddie for walk*—but the stroller was still on the porch, which meant Maddie was in the BabyBjorn carrier, strapped to Sarah's chest, where she would probably be sleeping by now. Which was fucked up because this made a transfer to the crib impossible. Maddie *never* transferred from the carrier. A strap tapped her nose, her foot became tangled, or maybe it was just the fact that she was listening to your heart, and to suddenly be taken away . . . Babies don't need a lot. Or, they need too much. Adam didn't want to care about this anymore. He didn't want to care about *any* of this anymore. He wanted to have conferences to plan for and impressions to track. A/B messages and image tests. Cookies and landing pages and follow-up emails to please post a five-star review. He wanted to be bored and to lament being bored. He wanted to look forward to time off and bitch about his coworkers. Because right now, his coworker was his baby.

His world was too small. He *needed* to talk to someone. He was vibrating, and it seemed as though the frequency was turning dangerous.

"Hey, Siri, call Jamie."

Jamie. The other friend from the so-called "tripod," the three of them going back to freshman year of college. His best man. Friends forever. He hadn't spoken to him in months. Jamie lived in New York, worked some job in finance Adam didn't understand and owned a closet full of suits. He was married to a stiff, formal woman from the city with family connections and traditions of going to the Hamptons. They didn't have kids, not yet, but they were trying. Adam used to, before he got fired, see Jamie once a year when Lostine Windows sent him to Design-Glass in the city. Usually a stilted lunch and then one night of debaucherous drinking in upscale bars high in buildings with elevators that shrugged off gravity at tremendous speed. That or down low, in cellar-accessed speakeasies known only to the rich: dirty chic. Then on to tumbly group calls where they shouted at Liam to get away from the fucking fish and come see them!

But Jamie didn't answer either.

"You have reached the phone of Jamie—"

Adam hung up. It didn't matter. What would they talk about anyway? Parrot back and forth the last thing they heard on one of NPR's constellation of podcasts? *Wait, wait, don't tell me, I heard it too.*

Sarah. Was she, right this minute, off somewhere with Kemp? No, not with their baby too. He imagined Maddie asleep on her chest as she walked the neighboring blocks and looked in lit-up windows at families doing better than them. They were all doing so much better than them! Adam knew he would be up late again, pacing with Maddie, begging her, at wits end, to *just fall asleep*.

He went to the fridge. A fingerful of peanut butter, a fingerful of honey. Then he shoved them both back in the fridge, behind the milk, the Brita, and the wilting, aspirational scallions. He'd like to be the kind of SAHD who cooked with scallions. Instead he was hiding his jars of honey like Winnie the Pooh. From himself? From Sarah?

Adam didn't have anyone else to call, which was absurd. Not too long ago, he'd been in college. Awash in connections. The ant had made it to the white wall above the cabinets. It was trucking toward the ceiling.

He couldn't call his parents. They were stiff, stunned-seeming people who had moved to Bend when they retired and were obsessed with their health. They drank nonfat lattes in cafés in biking spandex, helmets still on. They sent him articles about retirement funds and updates on his high school classmates. He had assumed they would want to visit Maddie more often, but they seemed fine with a holidays-and-birthday cadence. His sister, who lived in San Francisco with three kids of her own in a building with a doorman, was an equally dire prospect. Long stretches of silence, him busily trying to fill the holes with *so* and *well* and *anyway*.

He googled himself. There was nothing, in that there were a thousand things. Adam Coopers all over the place. None of them special.

He put on music. A mix ready-made for him by iTunes. Nothing to think about there. He didn't even know what he liked anymore. All the songs he knew by heart were from high school. High school! He kept skipping to the next song. It was all trash.

Adam tried to find a podcast and started cleaning up. Slick transitional music. Thanks to BreakFaster Cyclone for our theme music. The Woozy Sock Company for their support. He'd never once bought a product because of a podcast ad. How were these things making money? But maybe he should start one? Used to be everyone had a novel in them. Now everyone had a season or two.

"Hey, Siri," he said, a whim made reality in the space of a breath. "Call Ali."

The phone rang and rang until it rang out.

"You have reached the number 323—" Ali's phone informed him in the robotic voice of someone who hadn't set up their voicemail. But Ali *had* set up her voicemail, hadn't she? He had called her once to tell her that the lights were on in her car. Her message was something breezy and cool. *Hey, this is Ali—you know what to do.* So her phone had been reverted to factory settings . . . not a good sign. But, no, Kemp was gone, he reminded himself. The 4Runner was gone. Kemp had walked to his truck and left. And Ali's message could have been changed since he'd last tried. New phone, who this? It didn't *have* to mean anything.

The ant had made it to the ceiling. Antigravity feet. And then, incredibly, it fell. Adam tried to locate it amid the scatter of his kitchen floor, the desiccated grape halves, the petrified cheese puffs, the dirt, the dirt, the dirt. But it was camouflaged too well among the resting mess, and besides, there was a hot, metal smell. He looked at the stove. The burner was on. High heat, pan emulsifying from shiny black to dull white. He'd set it on the flame to dry it after he'd washed. He'd forgotten to turn off the burner. For all of his obsessive worrying, this had somehow slipped. He stared at it. *What did he do, did he do something, what did he do?* Adam was still staring when the door opened and he startled back, knocking a mug from the counter. It shattered at his feet.

"Oh," Sarah said, whispering. "Did I scare you?"

She was red-flushed. Maddie was, like he'd guessed, asleep in the carrier.

"It's no big deal," he whispered, turning off the stove and stooping to the task of gathering up the shards. "The fate of every mug."

"Thank you for cleaning," she said; she had noticed the clean dishes and the clear counters. The floors were next, but the floors were always next and rarely ever got done.

"I—" He looked up from his work, his hands full of sharp points that could cut him. She was beautiful and looked a little scared, and he was reminded that she didn't like this either, their constant tension. Their fights. Nobody wanted this. Nobody got into a marriage thinking they would end up with something like this. *What is going on?* he wanted to ask her. *What in the world is going on? You and Kemp?*

"I'm sorry about Maddie," Sarah said. "She was awake, and then I went for a walk. Honestly, I just wasn't thinking. This mom at school, she's really upset about something. It's just been one of those days. I needed air."

"It's OK," Adam said. He pressed the lever on the trash can with his toe, setting the broken mug inside.

"I'm just going to try," Sarah said, rocking back and forth in the dorky one-two beat all parents use to keep babies somnolent. "Maybe we'll get lucky and she'll transfer."

She tiptoed to Maddie's room elaborately, like the Grinch creeping over to presents under the tree. It was funny. *She* was funny. Especially with her body. A startling thing to learn when they first started sleeping together. For Adam, until Sarah, sex had been a poorly performed fanfic of porn. Each person played the part of a wild sex animal. God, we are so good at this! Aren't we so good at this? You like that? That's fucking. That's *fucking* right there. Instead, Sarah had laughed, and teased, and clenched at the wrong times to make a joke of them, of taking anything too seriously. Once, she had impersonated a debauched French aristocrat named Mademoiselle Flor, demanding increasingly wild things from Adam involving cheeses and wines. It was, to that day, the hardest he'd ever laughed. Or came. Where had that woman gone? Vaporized in the heat of maintaining this life.

She disappeared into the room. The white noise started up, a loud hush, and Adam loaded the last of the dishes into the washer and wiped down the last counter. Sweeping crumbs into his hand, a wet handful, he dashed them into the sink. Good luck! They hadn't eaten dinner, and he considered, suddenly, that he could get takeout from White and Green. Their revelatory Khao Soi. That they would sit at their kitchen table and drink wine and eat good food. Maybe he would even take out the battered deck of honeymoon cards from Costa Rica advertising some eagle-themed beer and add to the ongoing gin rummy tally. One million to one million and one. Bic marks on the inside flap of the card box. The tableau was so clear that he experienced it. It made him wonder at how much time he'd wasted doing anything else. Early nights to angry bed. Ignoring her to watch a meaningless November Blazers game. Just because he suspected his wife of something didn't make it true. He could have this all wrong. Crispin was after Ali, not his wife.

He hung up the dish towel and put on his coat just as Sarah was coming out of Maddie's room having—a miracle visited upon us!—managed the transfer.

"Where are you going?" she wondered, a little weakly. *Are we fighting still? Are you storming out? What do you know? Are you sending a message?*

"I was just thinking we could get some takeout," he said. "Have a little night of it. A date night. I . . . I just don't feel like I've gotten to hang out with you lately."

She smiled and he saw he had managed to surprise her. She would forgive his unwashed body, his baby-piss-stained clothing, his indiscretions, past, current, and future. And would he do the same for her? He decided right then, so long as she did him the mercy of never telling him, he would forgive her.

"That sounds nice," she said. "Just me and you."

Adam left the house and looked back. When he was certain the curtains in his home were drawn and that he wasn't being watched, he went and knocked on Ali's door. Three loud raps. And then he waited, feeling hurried. If Sarah bothered to check, she would see him there, and the bubble of grace they had managed to float between them would burst. But he had to do this. Now. Turn off the radio in his mind. Get back to his real life. The one that mattered. If he was really going to move beyond all this, he had to cross this off. He would ask one of her roommates where Ali was, and then the realization that she was missing would dawn, and *they'd* take the next steps and take the responsibility from his hands.

Kemp had left. His SUV was gone. But maybe Ali had been with him? Her voicemail had changed. Kemp must have destroyed her phone because he didn't want to be tracked. *What had he done, did he do something, what had he done, did he . . .*

Adam knocked on the door again and then held the wrought iron railing and peered around the side of the house, where he'd seen Kemp pee just that morning (it seemed eons ago), where he'd stood holding the shingle that afternoon.

"Come on, come on," he said.

He should have known. They had been too easy on Kemp. Adam had *never* trusted him. This could be the crucial time when there was still a chance of saving Ali. Wasn't that what they always said? That if you didn't break something in the case within the first few days, *hours,* then the chances of the victim being found alive dropped steeply?

Adam remembered the day he'd met Kemp. How he'd pulled Ali to his side like he was sure Adam and Sarah were going to try and snatch her away. How he bragged about his job at Logicstyx. Adam should have spoken up sooner, when Kemp tumbled from his SUV and peed on her house. He should have called the police or opened the door and shouted at him to go home. It was *not* normal behavior.

Adam hammered on the door again. The door swung in, and there stood Jay, Ali's roommate, in a bathrobe, pink-cheeked.

"Adam?" she said. "What's going on."

"I'm worried about Ali," he said.

"Ali? Why?"

"She didn't go to work today, and, well, I saw Kemp around last night, and it just doesn't seem normal. He *peed* on the house."

"He what?"

"Like a dog," Adam said.

"But Ali's home."

"What?"

"She's in her room." Jay closed the door a little and called up the stairs. "Ali? Adam's here. He says he's worried about you."

There was nothing for a moment, and Adam wondered if this was how Jay would discover that there was something wrong too. He imagined how it would factor into her story, one she would tell for the rest of her life. The moment she realized something was wrong. *And the whole time, I just thought she was upstairs, in her room . . .*

But then he heard a door close, the steps creak, Jay whispering back and forth with someone, and Jay padding off, back to her bath. The door swung wide again, and Ali peered around the edge, full and alive.

"Ali?" Adam said.

"I know, I know," she said, blushing. "I look terrible. I went camping and, Jesus, I got attacked by mosquitos. I'll never go again. Why do people love camping?"

"But I called you and you didn't answer," he said. "Your voicemail isn't set up, and your room was all muddy."

"The shed flooded. It caked all my shit, and when I packed, it got everywhere." Ali stopped, tilting her head. "But, Adam—how do you know my room is muddy?"

PART 3
A Person of Interest

Never again

My hands are shaking. This is getting to be too much. He showed up at my bus stop today. It was fucked up, and I'm not going to lie, I was a little scared. You could just kind of see something in his eyes, you know? Like, some serial killer vibes. I wasn't alone, but you know how it is with people now. This other guy who was waiting for his own bus, he was just into his phone. Even though my ex was being real intense, demanding that I take him back, give him another chance, or whatever, this other guy just kept staring at his phone. You could tell that he was just hoping that it would all go away. He didn't want to get involved in anything. Nobody ever wants to get really involved. You know, people seem to care a hell of a lot more about tracking their order for a new pair of shoes than what's happening in real life, right in front of their eyes.

He tells me he can change. That we can go out more, that we can have dates, we don't have to just Netflix and chill. He's telling me that I have to give him another chance. Like it's written into some kind of contract. And he hugged me. I didn't want it, so I pushed him away, and I just ran. I was so scared. And my coworker, she's telling me to call the police, but what am I supposed to say? My ex hugged me too hard? And it's got me thinking, like, maybe him and Window Boo across the street are the same crazy, just different flavors. Like, all that striptease through the windows . . . what would he have been capable of if that had ended wrong? Like, how can he have that *IN OUR AMERICA LOVE WINS* bullshit in his front yard and then be a nasty peeping Tom every night?

Anyway, I went camping by myself, if you can believe that. I needed to get away from *both* of them. And I tell you this: NEVER AGAIN. I was DESTROYED by bugs. And when I come back, guess who's lurking? Guess who's somehow spied into my room? Fucking neighbor boy.

They're both the same kind of creepy, just different volumes.

POSTED BY UNKNOWN AT 7:07 PM
0 COMMENTS:

23

Ali

Aᴌɪ ʀᴇᴍᴇᴍʙᴇʀᴇᴅ ɪᴛ as an accident of timing. Not thinking about her windows, or who might be looking in them, she'd just come out of the shower and was caught up in the daily back-and-forth waver of if she had been up in Oregon for too long. Caught up in her head. Long, dry, sweaty August days. She was so bored. Should she move home to LA? Should she give up on making her prints? Artistic ambition. Ha! She was a receptionist with an Instagram account and an anonymous Internet diary. She'd come up to Oregon to pursue her dreams. Portlandia, place where the young go to retire, artsy and free. But nothing was going her way. She should start applying for something with a 401K, health insurance, and company off-sites.

Then she looked up, only wearing her towel, and there was Adam. The neighbor she'd become somewhat friendly with. Waves and head nods. Flirts at the Fourth of July block party. Him and his wife. Welcoming her to the street, giving her their old heater last winter when the one in her room crapped out. The hellos, the texts about car alarms, the bitching about Tina and her floodlight. But now, that good neighbor vibe was gone. His eyes, they landed in her body like two marbles down her esophagus, just slightly too big to swallow. She had a moment of fear that she might choke. Her first instinct? Turn away, slam the curtains closed, wallow in the embarrassment that this was somehow *her* fault. That had been the day when she and Candice were called up to clean out a conference room used for a company party the night before. They had found, no joke, human shit in one of the trash cans. Something somewhere had gone public, and the boys had taken it a little too far celebrating their fresh wealth, their supervisor explained with an indulgent little smile. Baby millionaires. They work so hard that, sometimes, they need to blow off steam.

She was finding that this life up here would use you the same as life back home.

She looked across the space between their houses. She saw that he would take whatever she chose to give, and so she controlled him. She controlled *this*. Her fingernails on her own skin, a scrape, a shiver, a doppel of goosebumps down her clavicle, between her breasts, nipples hardening. She went slow. She went so slow. Even as she saw what he couldn't—what gave this whole practice worth. That Sarah was stirring in the floors below. At any moment, she would ascend. *This* was the point. *He* was the bait. Which made her the fisher. Night after night, she pushed him further, more, inch by inch. She found within her body a capability she hadn't known she held. Adam could be any one of them. He was all of them. He was this place. He was her frustration. She could let him be caught. Any one of these nights and she could make it all come crumbling down. A low punch, tingle and slide. A way to get back. A way to be something else.

But now, cleaning up her muddy room, she wondered if she had misplayed her hand. He'd shown up at her front door. Had he climbed the laurel and spied into her window? Was he the reason she'd found it left open to the cold? These men. These Kemps and these Adams. They were too much.

24

Evie

N o, I wasn't worried. Not at first at least. To be honest, it wasn't all that uncommon for Crispin to disappear for a few days. He didn't technically even live with us. He just stayed from time to time. He's a grown man. The business trips, the house he owns, coding off-sites at some Airbnb. There were plenty of places he could skip off to. You can't expect me to know where a grown, adult man is *all* the time. That wouldn't be an appropriate relationship, would it?

After all, even if he was supposed to come over for dinner, even if Mike seemed to think he was expected because they were going to talk about Logicstyx, *I* certainly don't remember it. I like to give him space. Usually, it's not a formal arrangement. He's welcome to drop in for dinner any night of the week. We're his family unconditionally. We love him unconditionally. No matter what he does. Rude doesn't enter the equation. He's welcome to take what he needs. If he doesn't show up sometimes, he doesn't show up sometimes. I give him a safe place to be *all* of himself. Even the ugly parts.

We are a culture of constant check-in but very little care, don't you think? Parents look up from their phone long enough to ask what their kid is doing on *their* phone and that's somehow enough. Most are just trying to shield themselves from emotional liability though, isn't that it? At the end of days that seem increasingly the same, sitting up on their phones, numb and number, they can say, oh, but I texted Johnny. I saw where he was on Find My Friends. I liked his latest post. I *care*. I *actually* care.

No, I've never had Crispin on Find My Friends. He never gave me permission, and I was *fine* with that. He wanted his privacy! He *should* want his privacy!

But what I'm saying is that it's absurd to think I *didn't* care just because I didn't have my finger in every pot. *That's* what I'm trying to explain. Your questions seem to imply that I didn't do my job as a mother. What it actually is, is that we've grown uncomfortable with real care as a society. Real communication not mediated by glass. Anything that forces you out of that gauzy digital cocoon. Have you seen the houseless problem in our city? We have a real empathy issue these days. And yet we drive right on by, listening to our podcasts.

I prefer to *talk* with my son. To *know* him. And that won't come, I swear to you, by demanding he check in once a day. Doing it through a screen. Call or text! Glass and pixels are just a modern way to make a mirror.

Don't you think everyone needs space from time to time? My son is no different. He's an incredibly intelligent young man, and for all the power and opportunity it gives him, sometimes he *needs* a moment to breathe. Even if he won't admit it. With the breakup and the stress at Logic-styx, I was just trying to give him that space.

No, no, no. He was *allowed* to be ugly with me.

I never held it against him. A mother's love is stronger than that.

25

Ali

Two DAYS AFTER they broke up, Ali left work and found Crispin waiting for her on the bench of her bus stop. Which, he shouldn't have been. She'd begged off early. It was only one in the afternoon, and he usually worked well past six. Besides, he was supposed to be in Seattle at a company off-site. But there he was. How long had he been there? He couldn't have known that she was leaving early, but somehow he had.

The moment she saw him, huddled on the bench, she tried to turn away, but he spotted her. She only wished herself smaller. To shrivel up into old age and disappear from his attention. Be less and less again until there was nothing he could grab, not even enough to see. Just a mote, a speck, a passing thought from before.

"Ali, wait—I just want to talk."

She sighed, looked out at the gray, washed day. What were her alternatives? Call an Uber? She would have to wait for it to arrive. Walk to the next bus stop? He would follow. Or, she could walk all the way home, a journey of almost four miles.

"Crispin, aren't you supposed to be in Seattle?" She had waited to break up with him until he was due for a business trip, thinking it would make things go easier. Space, time, work.

"That doesn't matter," he said. "They don't know shit. They want to pretend like we're some foosball and scooter company."

Ali was always taken aback by his rage at Logicstyx, the place that would soon make him astronomically rich. She'd been first attracted to him because he'd seemed to be everything she was lacking. Professional, stable, on a path. Now his hair was wet, his clothing soaked. But the squall had just come and gone. She and Candice watched it raging from their desk, taking videos and laughing. Like a dump truck in the sky had beep, beep, beeped into place and let loose the deluge. She'd sent the video to her sisters back in sunny California, asking them why they didn't want to come and visit her in Oregon.

Girl, I'd be washed away!

Then she put up her hood and stepped out into it, bouncy at the prospect of meeting Mel Sweetney. Another design job, another step in the right direction. *That's* why she was leaving so early. She had a meeting with her future and she didn't want to be late. She planned to get home with enough time to dial in her portfolio. But the rain. It had come and gone in ten minutes, less. Which meant Kemp hadn't been waiting long, because he was wet too. It meant he had run through it just to catch her. So, either she was unlucky or . . .

"Crispin, are you *tracking my phone*?"

"I just want to know . . ." he started, but then another man huddled into the bus shelter too, collapsing an umbrella, shaking free the drips.

At least there was that. They were not alone.

"I asked you a question. Did you do something with my phone? How did you know I would be here?"

"No, of course not, I just . . ." Crispin stood and took a step closer, one glance at the other man, who was already cozily zombied by his phone, and lowered his voice. "I just want to . . ."

But Ali had stepped away, a bodily memory, *danger, danger, danger*. She could placate him, a haunted chorus brainwashed into her since she was just a little girl. What's the harm in humoring him?

"Ali, I just want to know why I'm unlovable," he whispered. His voice was brittle. He was crying. He was actually crying, something he'd never done before, not even when she dumped him. Her heart turned a little at the vulnerability, the cracked-up look at his inner workings.

"You're not unlovable, Crispin," she told him, even though he seemed intent on proving exactly this. "Of course you aren't. There are lots of women—I mean, most of my friends think I'm crazy for breaking up with you. They thought I'd hit the jackpot. It's just, it wasn't going to be me, was it? We weren't even together that long and it wasn't working."

He stared at her, his beautiful blue eyes, and for a moment she thought he was going to be honest and agree. But something hardened within him instead, a cementing agent added to the slurry of his emotions.

"Exactly," he said, smiling in an odd, off-kilter way. "It wasn't that long, so you don't know for sure. Not for sure. If you had problems with how we spent our time, if it was too much in your bed or too much Netflix, you didn't exactly give me a chance to change, did you? *That's* not fair." He was saying it as though he were reminding her of some set of rules agreed upon by every dating person in the world. "You *have* to be fair."

He grabbed her, took her into his body, up against his wet coat. His breath, her neck. That familiar smell he had, minty and slick, woodsy and clear, and it was a hug, it was an assault. She pushed, but maybe not hard enough. Maybe she should have yelled, screamed, clawed. *Why didn't you fight?* Maybe she should have told him all of the worst things she had saved up. That in fact, yes, he was unlovable. That he was a puddle claiming to be a lake. That his smile was creepy, his laugh buffoonish, his wealth limp. That his hairless chest was disgusting, that he wasn't funny, that even all the Logicstyx money in the world wouldn't change his appeal. And maybe—there was someone else right there, after all—she would have been helped. That stranger would have looked up from his phone and helped her. Surely, he would have. Look up from your phone. This was real life. It was so much more serious than whatever it was he held in his hand. *See me, value me, protect me.*

Or maybe he wouldn't have.

She pushed against Kemp but he held her easily, and her breathing was too short, too small. She didn't want to push her hardest because what if she did and it wasn't enough? Hold a little bit back, just the smallest amount. And she felt, deep within her, tumblers flipping into place and a bargain being made. Just this. This last thing. She could give him this. It wasn't too much to ask, after all. A hug. And then they would be done, forever. Of course, he would get over it. They all would. That was the nature of life: getting over it.

"I could change your mind," he whispered into her ear. "I know I could make you change your mind."

"No, Kemp, I—"

But he continued to hold her too tightly and she tripped, to the side, and brought him with her. A few stumbled steps, a gasp, a little noise of terror, and the man waiting under the shelter looked up, owlish, wondering, *Is there something wrong? Hold on, what am I seeing here? Should I do something? I hope to God I don't have to do something. Like, will I have to use my hands?*

And then Kemp let her go and she turned away, fear in her throat, her knee pulsing with a twist. Too much water in there. Springtime for pain. A blooming of hurt.

"It can't be over," he said.

"It is."

Ali ran. Galloping and impish with her throbbing knee. Back into the lobby. Wet shoes against a squeaky floor, businessmen adjusting slim knots in their ties, Candice on the phone. She saw Ali coming and hung up, then came around the side of the desk and held her shoulders, leading her to a chair at the edge of the lobby. Ali told her about the encounter with Crispin. The strange smile, the hug—the assault?—the words. "We should call the fucking cops," Candice said.

"And what would I tell them?" Ali said. "That he smiled at me wrong? That he hugged me too tight?"

"Well, I'm here for you," Candice said.

"What am I even doing here?" She'd come to Oregon to make art, to make her own life, to get away from the expectations of her family. How had it been reduced to something so small and squirmy? "I don't know what to do with all of this." Ali breathed in deeply, down to the very bottom of her lungs, oversaturated and woozy.

"I don't know," Candice said. "But if you just put this on your blog but don't do anything about it? Nothing is going to change."

Ali's knee hurt. It had twisted wrong. All of this had become twisted and wrong.

26

Adam

WHEN ADAM HEARD Sarah on the stairs, he put his phone away and picked up his book. Thin pages. A dramatic, historical novel about a king and his counselor and deception, double-crossings, scandalous affairs. He rubbed his feet together. The words were hunched beetles conga-lining across the page. Sarah opened the door, and he kept his eyes on the book but watched her on the margins.

She surveyed the bed, the shelves next to it. Tissues, glass of water, her Kindle. Her phone charger, her journal, her retainer. The body pillow and weighted blanket. The little bowl of pills, a candy dish of melatonin, valerian root, and Benadryl, in case sleep put up too big a fight. She slid under her covers, pulling the weighted blanket to her chin, and put her retainer over her teeth, plastic clicking in with the precision of a latch catching.

"Pretty tired?" Adam said, as nonchalant as he could manage. He wondered if they might have sex. He needed *something.* To celebrate? To distract him from embarrassment? Ali was OK. Kemp had driven away. And who knew if whatever he suspected had happened between Sarah and Crispin actually had? Maybe the worry, like most worries in his life, had been in his head. A bad dream you wake up from.

"Yeah," she said. "It's been a long day. I'm . . . There's a lot to wrap my head around."

Adam imagined hunters back along his ancestral lines lusting through the forest after a doe. His hand ached with desire to reach across, to touch her. They'd had dinner together, which had been pleasant if not delightful.

He put the book away, then turned off the lamp. He performed each action with deliberate choreography that he hoped conveyed a mindfulness. And the room fell backward into dark. Those thick curtains they'd bought once upon a time when they thought they might co-sleep with Maddie. Sensory deprivation. But no, keeping baby with them just meant *nobody* slept. Her little body grappled with dreams between them, hungry and noisy. He remembered how momentous it felt, the first night Maddie slept in her own room. They had been freed. Everything the next morning was clearer and brighter.

He lay there, eyes wide, looking up at where he supposed the ceiling was. How can you really tell if things stayed where they were when you couldn't see them? You had to check. You always had to be checking. Would Sarah pick up on his smoldering energy? Fucking Ali. Fucking Kemp. He wanted to fuck his wife.

He reached out to touch her even though he'd promised himself he wouldn't. Self-flagellation. I who have messed up shall await your blessed finger. Here walks the pervert. Her arm shied away, the tentacles of a sea anemone you poked in a tidal pool.

"I have my retainer in," she said.

"And that's the final word?"

"I think I might be getting sick."

"Come on," Adam said, rubbing her arm. "If we just cuddle."

Sarah picked up his fingertips like he was a toddler touching a display case. And honestly, he should know better. She dropped his hand over his own chest, and he must have made a sound, though he didn't think he'd made a sound.

"Oh, so you're upset because I'm feeling sick?" Sarah wondered.

"I never said that."

"It's clear, Adam. With you, everything is so completely clear. And now that Ali *isn't* tied up somewhere after all, *now* you want to fuck me?"

So she had seen him go and talk to Ali. So did that mean their dinner together had been an act? Maybe he should get up, storm out of the room. Go to the bathroom and jerk off to videos on his phone—all the technological advancements in the world coinciding into a rectangle of flesh; no wonder we hated ourselves—but he wasn't sure who that would punish, exactly. First, he wouldn't be able to stamp his feet, slam doors, or yell without waking Maddie. Second, after the brief hiccup of pleasure—gauzy toilet paper, sweaty armpits—he'd be a man in a cold bathroom with his sweatpants around his ankles and his ass on the lid of a (probably) dirty toilet seat.

"You know what, yeah, I want to fuck you, OK?" Adam didn't like the emotion in his voice. But how could

he help it? He might cry. These last few weeks . . . "What's
so wrong with wanting to fuck your wife?"

"I don't know, Adam." She turned away, like this was
going to be it, but then said, very quietly, "It would be nice
if you liked hanging out with me, if it wasn't just about sex."

It hadn't always been like this, of course. When they
were first together, they were exactly how all of the movies
and the songs said they would be. And then, when they
were trying to have Maddie, it was endless. It was too much
sex, actually. Gym sessions. Good job, you. Glad you went
once it was over, but could you say you actually *liked* doing
it in the moment? Then they found out from the doctors
that they might have a hard time conceiving because of
this and that. Adam was never entirely sure about the biol-
ogy. He drifted when science came up, to Sarah's everlast-
ing annoyance. He knew only that he found himself one
Saturday in the clinic. It had felt wrong pacing the waiting
room and looking at all the paintings on the walls of wild,
unspoiled scenes of the world as it used to be—oceans and
forests, fog and sand, verdant, abundant growth—and
thinking that maybe, if they couldn't do it the way nature
intended, perhaps it was a sign. Not that they shouldn't
have kids, but maybe they needed to reconsider what having kids meant. Why were people so obsessed with having kids that came from *their* specific genetic tissue? Sure,
Darwin would tell you a lot about that, but why did it
carry still? Was there really all that much natural selection
being applied? Were old white men better suited, biologi-
cally, for the world? They certainly ruled it. But no. It was
the opposite, if anything. The fat, the bloviating, the delu-
sional would all be beaten to death with their golden toilet
seats in any kind of fair competition.

"How can you say that?" Adam wondered, looking up where, he knew, somewhere in the darkness, the dream catcher hung. "How can it only be about sex if we haven't had it in so long?"

"I didn't say that," Sarah said. "I mean, it's the only thing you want. That's what I mean. It takes me longer. You've never understood that. I want you to be *nice* to me. I want you to *connect* with me."

"Oh Jesus," Adam said.

"Adam, I gave you bids all day long. I told you how I loved you, I tried to empathize with you, I couldn't wait to come home and see you, and what do I get? You telling me to go feed my child? To take her off the shelf? Some insane theory about Ali being kidnapped? You checking up on Ali? I thought we were *done* with that girl. I thought we were *over* that."

"Here it is," Adam said. "You put up these impossible barriers. If I had known when we were trying to conceive Maddie that it would be the last time I was going to fuck my wife, I would have at least taken a video."

"You're being ridiculous and mean and misremembering," Sarah said coldly. "You couldn't give me Maddie even if we fucked all day long for ten years straight, and you know that."

Adam clenched his teeth until he felt tendons pop. What had been wrong with his sperm? He didn't know, exactly—hadn't *wanted* to know—only that they would have a better chance if the doctor collected it, if they did this and that to it, if they *gave it a little help*.

But maybe it was a sign, Adam concluded. A sign that only bad would come from his genetic contribution. Because what Adam had feared the most about having a baby was that he was just as likely to pass down the things he hated about himself as the things he liked. Why shuttle his obsessive thinking, his moral weakness, his webbed toes into another generation? Shouldn't they move to other options? Adoption or fostering? That would be better for the world, which, as everyone was saying, tongue in cheek or not, was burning. A little kid from some impoverished nation fairy-godmothered into the lap of this most privileged of countries currently on a pleasure barge floating toward a waterfall. How much money were they spending on this thing? And if not them, their insurance. Wouldn't it be better spent healing people who were already alive? Why did fertility as a medical specialization even exist? The world was afire and they were *paying* to pump in more fuel? It would be better for everyone involved if Adam and Sarah just lived excellent lives, kissing off peacefully in old age, goodbye, goodbye, without any attachments or concern.

"Oh, fuck you, Sarah," he said. "I *do* connect with you. Or I try. I got us takeout. Isn't that the kind of thing . . . I thought we *were* connecting. It can't be perfect all the time. We have a baby. It will be better when Maddie's older, but right now, you have to cut me some fucking slack. I swear to God, all you wanted was baby, baby, baby, and now that Maddie is here, you want everything we had from before. Well, it can't be like that, OK? I'm with her *all the time*, and it can't be like that."

Listen to me, she'd said, at the end of another barren month, sliding into a funk that would find her, sometimes, sitting in the dark in front of their closet mirror, pulling out strands of her own hair. *I need to explore this option.*

It wasn't in vitro. It was basically squirting a concoction of his sperm, somehow superpowered, into her vagina with a plastic syringe. And it felt like this was a car, Sarah's wishes were the hill, and there weren't any brakes. *Listen to me*. He'd go along with what she wanted. He would do anything to shake her out of it.

So the doctor called him in and said that if he wanted, Sarah could join him to help "procure the sample." What a wilting euphemism. Adam didn't want any "procuring," thank you very much. Sarah would only freeze him up. A few days before, after giving him head and coming back from the bathroom, she'd worried that he wasn't producing enough.

I swear, there wasn't that much in my mouth, she said.

What are you talking about? Adam wondered, annoyed because even this, again, always, wound its way back to fertility. Couldn't a blow job be just a blow job?

It was like if I bit a single pomegranate seed.

What the fuck?

You're not producing, Adam.

The room was horrible. The cold light, the chairs. God help him, the upholstered chairs. He plugged in his earphones and got to work. Only the earphones he'd grabbed on the way out had been through the wash and now squeaked at certain registers, the exact registers, it turned out, of a woman acting like she was in the throes of pleasure. He grew hard anyway, wincing against the squeaks, his coin-operated body, his dispenser of genetic material. He wanted to find something really good. He felt, perversely, like he *owed* it to his potential child. If he settled on some terrible clip of rubber boobs, stoic and immobile, he would have let this baby down, if a baby did indeed come from this ridiculous exercise. So he kept swiping through clips, the next one and the next one. They were all wrong, but it didn't matter because he couldn't help it. The sheer number of naked bodies was working in aggregate, and he was already coming, even as the clip he was on smash-cut to a close up of someone's something assaulting someone else's something. All while an anus rose in the corner of his screen like a mottled, alien moon and his earphones bansheed against his eardrums. The tip of his penis. The sharp edge of the cup. Snot down a window pane.

The miracle of life.

"Adam," she said into the blank roar of their marriage. "Adam, I *saw* you."

She saw him. Right. She didn't need to say any more than that. She saw how he'd gone across the street to Ali. His obsession through the window. He knew her complaint instantly: he'd made sure Ali was OK while neglecting his wife, who obviously wasn't.

"Yeah, well, I saw what Kemp was looking at last night with his dick in his hand," Adam said. "He was looking upstairs, wasn't he? He was looking into *our* window. He was looking at you. You tell me, why the hell would he be looking in our window, Sarah?"

"OK, here we go," she said. "Your intrusive thoughts are firing again. You got a theory about this too? You got some ugly fantasy playing in your mind? I don't have the energy for it, Adam. I just can't."

It was the worst thing she could have said to him because it was the thing he hated most about himself. And if she was rejecting his ugliness, then she was rejecting him. Because the moment that she had accepted him, monkey-mind and all, was the moment he knew that he loved her.

Adam drew the covers tight and measured out breaths in a strict regime, determined to never speak again. Soon, Sarah was snoring at his side. Maddie was in her crib, dreaming furiously, about to wake up, always about to wake up. Tina's floodlights illuminating the street, spotlighting Charlie's room. Ali was safe and sound. Kemp was somewhere doing Kemp things. This little life. For a moment, Adam had thought he'd seen the whole thing tilt. But he was wrong. It was a farce. You could see so much, and it might *still* come to nothing. The eyes were unreliable. Life will find a way. How boring. It turned out that he was just miserable.

He looked at his sleeping wife. How could she fall asleep? He wanted to grip her, shake her, take something from her. He'd loved her, once upon a time, hadn't he? Adam felt his face curl up like a grotesque Halloween mask, and soon, he was engulfed in tears. His face stretched to its limits. Skin pulled so thin, he might tear something. He kept it silent, the crying, but it was hard. He tasted pickles in his mouth. He bit down, teeth to teeth, face hot.

It felt as though he were burning. And then the thought came to him, unbidden, an evil spirit, of their house burning down. The flames licking upward from the kitchen, enveloping his life. The bubbled skin, the wailing baby, the coughing, the coughing, the coughing.

27

Sarah

THE NEXT MORNING, Sarah lay on her bed and poked her finger into her cheek. She told herself that she would stop when it became too much. But it never did. She had been doing this for weeks. Ever since Kemp had shown back up in her life, across the street, through Ali's window. Deep bruises. A tiny, red crescent moon. More makeup. Cakes of it. Did Adam notice? No, but Evie did. *Oh honey, you don't need any of that stuff. You're so beautiful on your own. If someone is making you think you need that stuff . . .*

Evie thought she was talking about Adam. And she was, in a way. But she was also talking about her own son.

Sarah wished her finger were sharper so she could spear right through to the soft sea-animal heft of her tongue. There were things that begged to be protected by a shell. Why were humans so soft?

She had called in sick and could hear Adam somewhere downstairs, trying to quell rioting Maddie. Her baby was wailing, and here she was—*bad mother*, she chanted to herself, *bad mother*. She poked until she gasped, until the pain clarified her actions, until a deeper system took over and she stopped in a blinding huff.

This was hard. This wasn't getting easier. She went to her closet and found the pink pants she'd worn to school yesterday, that hideous costume. She shot her hand into the pockets, lint and empty plastic eye-drop capsules, but there, at the bottom, was the little baggie of tablets she'd taken from Kemp. She swallowed one and looked up at the ceiling. The skylight. The dream catcher. Bitter, dissolving, she would soon be dissolving. She took another.

Last night, Adam had accused her of doing . . . exactly what she had been doing. Yet, she only felt rage. Like the squiggling pink worms or the scuttling potato bugs revealed when you flipped a decorative stone, some things were best left covered up. Sarah couldn't breathe, each intake less and less. A failing system. She turned over, her own stone, inert and awaiting whatever might happen. Pretended to sleep while her husband cried.

She told herself it wasn't her fault. It was Adam who had been fired from work for looking at porn. And then he became the man fired for looking at porn at work who also looked at the naked neighbor across the street. What would he do next? Adam needed to prove himself. *That* was their current relational contract. He had to do anything. No matter what. Because he was the asshole. He was *still* the asshole. And the asshole repents.

When Kemp began showing up in Ali's window, just for her, Sarah felt dishy and interesting. In control. Here was this woman who'd taken her husband away, and now Sarah held something over *her*. *Everything* Kemp was doing with Ali was in service of Sarah. And, God, she hated it. But, God, it purred down her back. She rolled over in the bed and stared up at the dream catcher. On and on, somewhere, Maddie cried.

"Adam!" she screamed. "Can't you take her somewhere?"

He answered something, but she didn't know what. She knew he was probably cursing her under his breath, bitter and resentful. Last night she had been cruel. They both had been. Their marriage was like the cherry tree in their backyard that only produced wormy fruit. Look at that abundance! *Everyone* commented on how pretty the tree was. Not a single one of them would like to eat of their fruit.

Of course she told Kemp about Ali and Adam's little window games. So he began dating Ali like an odd, creepy little gift, a way to pay for staying near. A cat turning up with a dead baby crow.

She allowed it. She just wanted to be taken away from her life.

What would happen was that she would sometimes get a text from one of his randomized numbers, telling her to go to the window. This was in the small hours, after Adam had shuffled out of bed to go and soothe Maddie downstairs. She would find Kemp there, in Ali's room, in *that* window. Only it was hers now. He had taken it from Adam, from Ali, and he gave it to her.

He and Ali might be watching a show on his laptop, or sitting up talking, but the moment Sarah opened the blinds, he would find a way to look at her. And whatever he did next with Ali, it would be for her. She'd been hurt, she kept reminding herself. *She* was the one who had been hurt *first*. Even as her mouth opened, as her body slid, as she gripped him red along his shoulders, down his back.

Afterward, they would text, little things, just what they could get away with.

Good movie
The best
Can't sleep
Me neither

She was so tired. She couldn't sleep because of Maddie, because she was mad at Adam, because, because, because . . . Kemp had drugs. He always had drugs. Sarah didn't even know what they were. In fact, she warned him off telling her. There was a line she wanted to hold, some kind of deniability about what she was willing to do. She just wanted to be taken away. To where she wasn't a mother, or a wife, or a teacher. She snuck out a few times—five, maybe six? Deep in the night when Ali and Adam were asleep. When Kemp managed to convince her. He never made her laugh, but he made her smile. And they walked up to Mount Tabor, where it was dark and it didn't matter. These were strange, floaty nights. Lying in the damp, the dirt, the trees, the cold. Small things on her tongue, lifting the weight only a little at first, and then entirely, birthing universes in the moments between blinks. He always pressed her that they should just keep on, go to his empty, echoing house, but she wouldn't relent. There was a line she was thinking about drawing, and staying outside, away from doors that locked and walls that hushed, was a start. Besides, she'd heard that walking in the forest was good for you, in part, because of the volatile organic compounds floating in the air. Your mental health. Your spirit. She told him this.

"No," he said. "It's got nothing to do with the volatile organic whatever and more to do with this."

And he kissed her, because he was so corny, and Sarah laughed at him. He had started to treat her like this delicate, glass thing. She wanted him the way he used to be, when they were first starting, the way he was with Ali through the window, but she couldn't tell him this. How could you ask for more when you wanted less? He pulled away, looking down past the ragged edge of his boyband flop. He was so young like that. He had feelings. Big Feelings that were easy to hurt. He looked at her like she had better come up with something very quickly, because it would go badly otherwise.

"I can travel," Sarah said. "If I just close my eyes, I can travel to any point in my childhood."

He laughed and fell into the dirt beside her, either because she had figured out the right thing to say or perhaps because she'd demonstrated how far gone she was. "You're high," he said. "You're just really fucking high and everything seems like it means something even if it doesn't."

Sarah closed her eyes and she was in college, at that party, sexy and young. She was with her parents at Sparky's Pizza, crying because she only got one slice, any more would be bad for her acne. She was swimming in a lake, trying to get across like she'd just seen her cousins do, the slimy pond grass lecherous on her legs.

She was with Maddie.

She was in love.

She was loved.

Those were the nights when she could get real sleep. Honest-to-God, dead-to-the-world sleep. Come back, emptied of the coil tightening, always tightening in her chest, and disappear into wherever you go when you close your eyes. The next day, she would find dirt under her fingernails and leaves in her hair. She would yawn through her morning meeting, her student Luke picking up on it and observing, like he knew what he was talking about, that maybe she'd had too much fun last night.

It felt, if not safe, then predictable. Not safe, not safe. She needed the feeling. Because what she had found, actually, was that when her life tilted, when her insides felt unworthy of the world, that if she outletted into something that was also ugly or dangerous, there was relief. She understood cigarettes. She understood driving a hundred miles an hour down dark roads. But when do you stop picking a scab? Not until there was blood, of course. So she poked her cheek. She pressed in, harder and harder.

Not safe, not safe.

She didn't feel safe.

Sarah went to the window and crouched, afraid she might topple over. It was still early for most of the world. Not even eight in the morning, but it was late by her standards. By now, the kids would begin showing up at the threshold of her classroom. By now, they would be seeing the sub, would be realizing that the day was a wash, would be bubbling among themselves with the gossip that Sarah was gone.

Across the way, through the skeletons of the sugar maples, she saw Ali's place, which was a little taller than her house but aching with its neglect. It was a piece of shit, frankly. It was losing roof tiles and chunks of the siding were sloughing off.

Last night—two nights ago?—Kemp had again forced her to meet him. One last time, he texted. One last time. She never should have gone. But Ali was out, her roommates were asleep, and he insisted they go into her house, that he had something he wanted to show her. Stupid her, she went. Stupid her.

Something lit up from the roof of Ali's house. *Somethings.* Crows. Black crows. So many of them that Sarah stumbled backward, fell across the foot of her bed, dizzy with the drugs hitting and imagining that the birds had seen her, that she was caught, tried, and found guilty. She looked up at the dream catcher and hummed the song. The drugs were pushing and pulling things apart. Because if she had a little white box, she'd put Jesus in. She'd take him out and kiss his face and put him right back in.

But what if she had a little black box? What would she do with that little black box?

28

Adam

Sarah's scream from upstairs echoed in his body. *Can't you take her somewhere?* The desperate *clawing* in it. The force with which it emanated. He honestly didn't know she had it in her. It wasn't even eight in the morning. Maybe he should have gone up there and checked on her, but maybe he was a coward. Or maybe he hated her. He just packed up Maddie as quickly as he was able, no bombproof kit, no break-in-case-of emergency packet of Cheerios or juice box. He just got out; he just left.

But when he emerged from the house, about to descend into his looping check, double-check, triple-check the door lock rat's nest, a Tesla glided up. Candy-red, gull-winged, snow-silent. Adam squinted and made out the unmistakable, upright visage of Evie Kemp. He knew she had a quiver of incredible cars to get to work in each morning. It was a point of gossip, one of many, a constellation of gossip by which to track the celestial Evie. Adam was impressed, though he didn't want to be. Capitalism had blue-checked this person.

The car yawned and Evie emerged in comically tall high heels, which were the rubbery pink of a fresh scar, and denim overalls Adam *knew* were fashionable but couldn't actually *believe* looked good. He was like a kid trying expensive wine. Notice the legs.

Evie was wearing a dark, blackberry lipstick that was the sulking purple of a bruise. She clipped over, careful in the slurry wet of the decaying leaves humped in his tree lawn. He suddenly felt embarrassed and unmanful. He'd never bothered with the leaves when they had been dry enough to rake easily. Now, like he had been doing for so many things, he would wait it out until nature took its due course. It all seemed more trouble than it needed to be. Print *that* on a T-shirt. SAHD merch from the off-key wail of his inner life.

"Adam!" Principal Kemp called out, which surprised him because, until this moment, he thought she didn't know his name despite being introduced to him multiple times at school and even in her own home. She had always feigned embarrassment and asked to be reminded again. Something they both understood to be an etiquette of power.

"Hi," he said.

"And Maddie." Principal Kemp leaned over his baby. Adam had the image of a Dementor sucking Daniel Radcliffe's face off. She would slurp Maddie's youth, use it to moisturize her own skin. He had the sudden urge to tell her what he'd seen her son do, what he suspected her son was still doing.

But no. That wasn't good. He needed to extricate himself from this. Adam inhaled. Principal Kemp smelled like a variant of vanilla you could never actually afford but which was called for in specific recipes. Premium domestic.

She wasn't evil; she was just rich.

"She's beautiful!" Principal Kemp said.

"We like to think so," Adam said and was immediately annoyed with himself. He sounded like his father. Did that mean he would one day move to some sunny, dry place and fossilize into a crust of date smoothies and Peloton sweat?

"Listen, I was so sorry to hear that Sarah has come down with a little something," Evie said. "So I brought her a smoothie. It's from Kure. It's the Lush Life, extra greens. It will have her back in fighting form in no time."

"OK," Adam said. "Thanks, but she's sleeping just now, and we're trying to get out of the house to give her some space."

"I *know* she's been having a hard time, and I just wanted to get her something to let her know I'm thinking of her."

"We're leaving," Adam said. "Can you leave it on the porch?"

"And have it warm up? No, it won't be any good then. I'll just pop right in, quiet as a mouse, and put it in the fridge."

"Oh, I—"

"It shouldn't go to waste, Adam." She pursed her lips, threw him a baby pout that he fumbled. What was he supposed to do? His heart was a racing sheepdog, and something whistled him back to attention. He should protect his wife from Evie's smothering care. But then he thought of the way Sarah had screamed at him and what she had said last night. His mind was befuddled, and Maddie was whining. She was strapped into the stroller. She wanted action, action, action!

"It's not a big deal," Principal Kemp said. "Look, you stay here with your baby, and I'll pop in and out."

Maddie really started to cry then, and he leaned over the stroller, trying to find a binky in one of the little side pockets stitched into the interior. When he stood up again, Principal Kemp was coming back out of his house.

"In and out," she said. "Just like I promised."

Adam stared at her for a moment, unsure of what had actually happened. He'd left the door unlocked and fucking Evie Kemp had been in his house! It was filthy inside. Stuff everywhere. Dishes in the sink. Clothing on the floor. Toys scattered, sharp and bright. He'd meant to do better. Which was the same as every day. Today of all days. And now he was going to the ducks to babble nonsense and hand Maddie pine cones and blah, blah, blah.

Evie met him with a calm gaze. He had left the door unlocked, and last night the stove was on. The broken mug. *What did he do, did he do something?* He could feel his agitation prowling, waiting to leap. He was being teased up, like a sticker on an old coffee mug.

"Don't worry, I locked up," she said.

"Oh—of course." Adam looked up into the rare, clear day. It had rained last night, but now? Not a cloud. A weak, blue shout formed the sky. It was mostly quiet, the occasional car passing on 43rd, the clattering sound of Mrs. Jenkins opening and shutting her door to let out her murdersome cat.

"We're going to the duck pond," Adam said dully.

"The duck pond!" Principal Kemp said, as if Adam had just come up with the most genius idea. *Good for you, you special, special star.* "Yes, of course, I remember when we used to do that! My Crispin *loved* the duck pond. God, he loved feeding them bread. Which I suppose you're not supposed to do now?"

Adam nodded. He knew what his line was. "I think it makes the ducks obese?"

He made a point of not looking at the door, but that was where his mind's eye was. *Had she really locked it? Was it locked? Shouldn't he just check if it was locked? Had she locked it?*

"Fat ducks, that makes sense," Principal Kemp said, nodding firmly, as if together they'd solved a thorny problem. "You know bread does the same to me!" She laughed and touched her flat side. She could be a fitness model. Still, he felt a deep desire to go along with whatever she said. God, did he love her? He was beginning to see why Sarah agitated over that sweater Principal Kemp bought her once upon a time. He'd underestimated what *his* wife was dealing with every day at work.

"Can you imagine?" she trilled. "People just *tossing* out the thing you most want, right in front of you? Of course we'd gobble it up! *Any* human would. There is *no way* we'd be able to turn our backs. We're just like animals. But we know better and better all the time, don't we?"

"We do?" Adam said.

"We do," she soothed.

"Right, OK." He pushed past her, up the steps, and tried the doorknob. It firmly refused to turn. She *had* locked it after all. And why not? This was bizarre. What had he been thinking? That she was up to something? Why did he believe that *everyone* was up to something? Ali was fine. Kemp was weird but had driven away.

Maddie squealed, and he jostled the stroller. "Just a second, just a second," he sang.

"I'm sure it's going to make her feel much better," Principal Kemp said, as though the smoothie had been *his* idea.

She pointed behind Adam. "They're bothered about something, aren't they?"

Adam turned and saw the crows. Ten, fifteen? They were perched on the wires. Twenty? Thirty? They were on Ali's roof. They were in the trees. More like fifty, or maybe even sixty? Their black eyes. Lifeless, shiver up and down. You could pluck the eyes out and roll them across the floor to skitter and bounce, hard as any marble. They gathered like this sometimes, Adam knew, for reasons ancient and ominous. Back when he had his job at Lostine Windows, biking along Naito twice every day, there were a few instances of thousands of crows gathering in the trees along the waterfront. Less a murder and more a massacre.

"Well, don't let me keep you," Principal Kemp said, urging him along. "The ducks are expecting you."

Adam was still looking at the crows. Their collating feathers. Little tip-tap steps readjusting their grips. Two of the birds lifted heavily from a long, jointed branch of the sugar maple growing in his front yard and made an obese parabola to gain Ali's roof, only *just* managing to make it instead of smacking into her window.

"Global warming?" he said, because the animals knew better than them. And he felt like he had to cover for the corvus. A malevolent deed. Creatures everywhere behaving oddly. His messy house, his flustered fowl. What we were doing to the planet seemed the most obvious culprit for almost everything, and nobody was doing enough to fix it. *He* wasn't doing enough! He hadn't even switched his power to renewable yet!

Evie held up her phone, taking a picture. So Adam did the same. It seemed important, just then, to have what she had.

"OK," Principal Kemp said, their bit of business done. "I'm sure we'll see each other soon. Mike and I are planning another get-together around the holidays. We had so much fun the last time."

"I wasn't there," Adam said.

"Oh, that's *too bad*," Evie said. "Everyone had a wild time."

And then she clipped back onto the street where the door to her Tesla retook her. Adam looked at the photo on his phone. All those birds. They *knew* something. Maybe he should just check again. *What did he do, did he do something, what did he . . .* The shingle. He'd slipped on a roof shingle. He could climb up the laurel but this time not stop at Ali's room. He could go all the way to the top.

Instead, he sang to Maddie, already starting to run. "Buck, buck, bucking broncaroo!" He would start working out, he would be better, he would change. Starting *now*. This instant. He left the Tesla, the crows, and the strange, compelling woman behind. As he ran, Adam remembered something Sarah had told him once. *Kemp keeps control by making you doubt everything.* And Adam himself didn't know if he was running from her, or from the whole, ugly truth that was just beginning to dawn in his head.

29

Evie

H OW DO WE know we're alive? Here's a simple test.
The next time you hear someone whistling a tune,
maybe you're in your backyard, in a spot of sun, and your
neighbor doesn't know you're out there, but you can *hear*
him songbirding, find the tune in your mind and practice
behind your lips. And then, just a whisper, so quiet, so the
neighbor will never know, hum along.

Do you feel that shiver? Can you barely get through?

That's one way.

That was Crispin for me, OK? He was the only thing in
the world that could make me feel alive. But Ali, and Sarah,
and whatever it was that he had gotten himself involved
with had taken that away. He wasn't himself anymore. And
his boss was calling because he still hadn't shown up, and
now his work wasn't being pushed to the servers anymore.
Then Sarah called in sick. It just didn't make sense. So I
went to her house, expecting to maybe find them together,
get to the bottom of it, but I found her husband instead.

Of course I found her husband instead. I had forgotten, or maybe I never knew, that he didn't have a real job anymore.

Still, I wondered. I needed to find out more. So I waited until Adam was gone, around the block, taking his little girl to the duck pond. He was running in heavy sweatpants and a huge, stained sweatshirt. What an odd man. Did you get that impression too, when you talked with him? Did it seem like something was a little . . . off?

No, I don't have the photo of the crows anymore and I didn't post it. Why? Because if I did, then some natural-ist parent would chime in with the definition of the exact phenomenon I was seeing and then suggest that maybe I should have them in to speak about it to the students. Jesus. Instead, I found a post from Mel, an illustrated plac-ard for a rally in two weeks' time on the waterfront, ironi-cally designed by Ali (the entry I'd given that girl). Let's change the world 👏👏👏, I wrote below.

I checked the mirrors and scanned the street. This close to my school? High chance some parent would be around and recognize me. I got out and went around to Sarah's backyard. I had unlocked the back door when I brought in the smoothie. I went straight in. No hesitation. You see, you have to be decisive. All it takes is a moment. I'm not proud of my actions, but I needed to see if I was right. I needed to protect my son. A mother always knows. Somewhere deep down, a mother always knows.

Inside the house—God, that house—annoyance burbled in my stomach. Spilled cereal, clothes half-folded on the dining table, shoes in the middle of the kitchen. A drunk, rabid raccoon could have been let loose. It was a disaster. But, in any case, silver linings, nobody would notice if I looked around.

No, I didn't have a plan. An opportunity had arisen. I was taking advantage of it to make sure my son was OK. I didn't know for sure about Crispin and Sarah, but I had suspicions. I noticed Sarah looking at him at my last party, and of course, I understood. Most young women look at my son like that. But then I saw him leading her away, upstairs. And then he starts dating Ali, who just happens to live across the street?

I know I was doing something that wasn't entirely right, but if you thought your son was in trouble, what kind of wrong would you try?

If Sarah *did* wake up and see me, I could say, *I was worried about you, I brought you a smoothie.* I took it out of the fridge, my prop, and carried it upstairs. Tippy-toes now, Lush Life sweating in my hand. The door to her room was already open, or I never would have . . . She looked like she was in trouble, to tell you the truth. She was sort of splattered there, on the end of the bed, in this threadbare T-shirt that didn't leave much to the imagination. Her skin was so pale. At first, for just a moment, I thought . . . but she was breathing. Small and shallow, but insistent. She looked so cold. She actually *was* sick. So I tugged the blanket over her and tucked her in. But the smoothie, some of it dribbled out of the straw hole. I didn't even think about it. I licked it away and set the drink on the windowsill. I forgot about it there, actually. Because out her window I saw Ali's house again. What a shithole. Crows on the roof. So many crows. A breeding thing? A funeral? I knew crows sometimes held funerals. How had my son, my one and only, spent so much of his time *there*. And all for this woman, passed out on her bed, breathing snottily through her nose. Has that ever happened to you? Have you ever watched someone you love make choices that were terrible for them? Did you try to stop them? Save them from their course? And if you did, how hard did you try? Are you able to sleep soundly? Did you do *everything* you could?

That girl Ali. That shack was probably teeming with black mold spores, and I worried that, many years down the line, Crispin's doctor might deliver a diagnosis of cancer. They would go down the list of potential causes, wondering where and when he had been exposed, never suspecting it had been his entanglement with a nobody, wannabe artist and the depressed woman across the street. The time spent in her house, maybe even looking out those windows, had led to his end.

I went into the closet. On a long rod hung all the outfits Sarah wore to school. I recognized most of them. It was a little pathetic how often Sarah wore the same things. Which made it all the stranger why she didn't wear the R13 sweater I'd bought her. I could have made her life so much easier. But there it was, hanging, pristine, tags still on. I'll be honest, I wanted to take it. Sarah obviously didn't deserve it. It was an expensive gift, but that wasn't the point. Acceptance was. If this was left unused, what did that say about our working relationship? Our relationship in general? Trust. I had thought we had it and I was mistaken. Early peoples gave gifts of food or tools as a way of conveying the promise of safety, a practice engrained for a millennia. The transaction credited both the giver and the taker. I and you, now together. But what if one reneged by hanging it, unused, in a closet? Does it send some kind of message or counterspell? It wasn't because the sweater didn't fit or wouldn't look good. I have an excellent eye for bodies.

Sarah would have been *stunning* in it. No, it wasn't anything more than a simple fuck you.

I went to the dresser and dug down through the drawers. One contained the underwear, balled rolls of delicate lace in bright, shot-up colors. I laid hands upon the pieces, the soft fabric, and slipped my fingers in deep. At the bottom, I found a lump. I pulled it out. A small zip case. I unwound it and found a white object shaped like a huge, frozen teardrop. Or the outline of an alien spacecraft. A vibrator. How nice.

And then I left her there. I closed the door and went back downstairs, but I left by the front door this time. I slammed the door, and the crows lifted from Ali's roof, en masse, like smoke into air.

30

Sarah

SARAH WOKE UP to a slamming door—her slamming door—and the shimmering buzz of her vibrator celebrating against her thigh, nestling into the fabric of her sweatpants. Had there been crows in her room? No, not crows, a crow woman. A swooping, spindly ruffle. Sarah had taken a tablet, or maybe two, from Kemp's little baggie. She was familiar with the effects. The colorful slide from sense. The way it could impose upon her imagination. But she had seen Evie in her room. And the vibrator winding down next to her. Evie had been in her room. Evie had been hunting in her room. She wanted something. She had left her a message.

But no. It was the drugs. She'd taken too much. Surely, it was her imagination.

Sarah sat up, sweating, sickly. She reached over and clicked off the vibrator and saw, there on the windowsill, a plastic cup from Kure. It was sweating, bright green. Thick and healthy. Maybe Adam had . . . but no. She stumbled toward it and noticed, at the base of the straw, the dark, purple bruise of Evie Kemp's favorite lipstick.

She *had* been there.

Now Sarah knew what that song from Sunday school meant. Jesus in the white box, Satan in the black. You kept both with you because to be human was to live between the two, always kissing one and beating the other back. Forever and always, amen.

She shouldn't have gone that night. No matter how much he begged. She wasn't Kemp's. She wasn't anyone's. She knew that. It had been stupid. Rash. But people get pushed and pushed, and sometimes it's no wonder they take a step. And sure, Sarah knew it was a useless game of faulty logic plenty of people engage in after they do something they regret, but she couldn't stop playing. If only I had done this, or that, or the other thing. Where did that start? How far back do you have to go to stop a bad decision? And even if you did, who's to say that something even worse might not have happened in its place? Kemp used to joke with her that he could use the Internet to find out anything about anyone. Sarah realized it didn't matter if he actually could or not. Just the fact that she believed he could was enough. She caught herself doing things like he *was*, in fact, watching her.

So when the text came through, Sarah had held off for as long as she could, but in the end, she dressed in the dark, by sense, fingertips and fabrics. She couldn't risk turning on the light and alerting Adam, down in the glider chair in the living room, up again with a fussy Maddie. And so she chose at random, in fact picking out the R13 sweater from Evie, until she brushed the tags and realized what it was. Later, she would see that she had put together a hideous combination. Pink pants, a light purple blouse. Will you be my Valentine?

She crept down the stairs, staying near the edges, tread by tread. Every squeak clenched her heart. Pain in her chest. She had her alibi picked out in case Adam woke up: *Oh no! I'm so sorry, go back to sleep! I forgot about this report on IEPs. There's no way around it.*

But he was asleep in the glider chair, over $1,500 worth of ease, their daughter on his chest. He'd wake with his back aching. Maddie's little mouth wide. And it was so sweet. Incredible. What a father he'd become. There were so many ways you could say he was failing, and Sarah had mentioned, or implied, most of them. But in this, in keeping her safe, in staying patient, in making her laugh—he was doing so well. It broke her in two.

She took out her phone and snapped a picture, these two beating hearts of hers, to capture her resolve fresh. She would protect *this*.

She crept outside, pulling the door closed behind her, feeling every creak and wince of wood and latch inside her body. She breathed from her mouth. It was so loud. How? A series of wind gusts. Then she crossed the street, feeling ridiculous as she moved in slow, choreographed motions so as not to trigger Tina's floodlight. Kemp was waiting for her, and the door seemed to open on its own, the sinister welcoming at the beginning of a ghost story. Finger to his lips. Smile (smirk?) playing there too. Ali was gone, but her roommates were still there. Why did Kemp want her *there*, in her house, risking all of this, when they could have gone to his place or for another walk up to Tabor. And yet, she went along because she felt safer like this. Here, at least, there were people close enough to come running. Sarah followed him up the stairs to Ali's room. It was filthy. Mud everywhere. Had something already happened?

"What the fuck is going on?" Sarah said.

"I think she went camping," Kemp said, waving away the mess. "It doesn't matter, I want you to look out this window. I want you to tell me what you see."

She looked; she saw her house, dark and empty. Though not empty, of course. It held Adam. It held Maddie. A scrape in her gut. The feeling of violent cleansing like the shuddering aftermath of a vomit. She could cry. It seemed so fake. Such an honest try. But Sarah feared they were doomed. They always said fake it till you make it. How much longer could she manage?

"My house?" Sarah whispered. She didn't like how little her voice sounded, a breeze whistling the edge of a peanut shell.

"I've been watching you," Kemp said. "My heart, in that window, and—"

"I know that. Fuck," Sarah said. She was trying on rage, frustration, anything to punch through this last bit. Blow the house down. "Don't you think I know that? I've been playing along too, haven't I? But it's done now, OK. It *has* to be done." She had the urge to press her finger into her cheek. Hard and pointed. Harder than ever. Lacquer nails finding red blood.

Kemp took off his glasses. He was always taking off his glasses when he had an important point to make. She didn't buy it. He was like an actor in a play pretending to be cold. Overdoing it by half. Huffing and rubbing his hands together over some flickering orange paper meant to be flames.

It was time for him exit the fucking stage.

"It tears me up," he said. "To think you're right across the street. That things should be different—that they're *so close* to being different—but they can't be. And why? Because we're scared? How long are we supposed to be scared? Life shouldn't be lived scared. We should *take* what we want."

"No, Crispin," she said. "It's exactly like it's supposed to be."

"Come on," he said. "You don't think that. We have something special; it's easy, me and you. From the very first moment I saw you, it was so easy. You felt that too. I know you did."

"I didn't," she said. "Maybe in a different life, but not this. This isn't . . . I don't think you love me either. You're so young; you're going to find someone new. I know you will."

"I don't believe you," he said. "What's in your heart, Sarah? Can you tell me that? Can you even see into it? Or is it too clouded?"

"This *has* to stop," Sarah said, wishing he would be quiet. Ali's roommates were presumably somewhere in the house, sleeping. "This is insane. What if someone sees me? Adam is sleeping, right now, in that chair in the living room. If he wakes up . . . if he . . . No. I'm leaving, and if you keep showing up, I'll . . . I won't care, OK? If you make it this hard for me, then I will do the hard thing too."

"This is the last thing," he begged, scratching the back of his head. "This is the very last thing. I want to show you something, and if it doesn't change anything . . ." There was desperation in his throat, thin and watery. Sarah had the image of her grandfather, who'd died, they said, because of fluid in his lungs. He just couldn't wake himself, and so he suffered what the doctors called a dry drowning. Pulmonary edema, stemming from a heart condition. Everyone said he had gone peacefully, but Sarah didn't think so. To wake up, already too late, in your warm bed, drowning.

"The last thing?" Sarah said, using a voice she often had to apply with Luke and other gifted kids over the years. Her register did two things at once; it petted their intelligence while also making it clear that you held the leash and all their play was used up. Because that was the thing with those who considered themselves special: you had to appease as you corrected, and you had to flatter as you limited.

So she followed him out of the window and up the trellis, laurel branches scraping her back, to the roof. They lay there, on the cement tiles, rough sandpaper to their backs, and looked up. The rain had quit, and the stars were out, every one, and she saw that Kemp had been right to bring her out there. It felt as if all those celestial bodies were just for them. A good effect. A nice try. As if they had gained the sky. A bit of magic that Sarah couldn't help but notice despite herself. Kemp, meanwhile, was anxious, fidgeting. He wondered if she was OK and worried that she was uncomfortable.

She looked at his thin, beautiful face, and something fell in her gut. She was sick. Twisted up. She realized it always had to have been Kemp because he *looked* like Adam. Younger, fitter, more energy, to be sure, and only in the right light, with the right squint. But, here it was. God, and it was pathetic. She was fucking a simulacrum of her younger husband. She was fucking her past. But the

second part of the realization was even worse. Kemp was
nothing like Adam. Because Kemp was dangerous.

"I wish this night could last forever," he kept saying.
"I just keep thinking about how this is a mistake, how
we belong together, and I wish I could stay right here,
forever."

He was crying, and soon it went beyond tears to an
ugly rictus of pain.

It struck Sarah how completely he changed. Now
he looked nothing like Adam, and almost like Maddie.
The complete abandon with which he gave himself to
his feelings. Nothing in him acknowledged anything
outside himself. No tempering for embarrassment or
politeness. The world pointed to him, and he expected it
to. Kemp's face stretched, desperate, frozen in the stalls
between sobs. He moaned, letting out a racked set of
breaths.

"I just wish. This. Whole thing. Could last forever."

"Kemp," she said, hushing him. Jesus. "Kemp, come on."

From below, white light bloomed. Tina's fucking
floodlights. The huff and shuffle of someone walking with
big bags, carrying cans. Tin Can Sam. It *had* to be him.
Up early. Go and get 'em. Sarah sat back on the roof, hand
over Kemp's mouth, until the footsteps moved on.

He tried to speak through her grip, tip of his tongue in
the shell of her hand.

"Stay quiet," she said, then let him go. "Someone is
going to see us."

"And that would be the worst thing? To be seen with
me?" He was being too loud. Dawn was approaching. Dog
walkers and runners emerging. They would look up and
wonder. She would be caught.

"Do you want to take something?" Sarah knew he had drugs. Kemp *always* had drugs. She saw the light from below, the other people nearby. She wanted him to quiet, to calm. And in no other state had she ever seen Kemp quite so much *himself*—there was no other way to consider it—than when he was high. He stopped cycling through identity and just floated.

Sure enough, Kemp broke from the loop of his sorrow and nodded, snottily. He pulled a plastic baggie from his pocket. Two dozen or so tablets at the bottom. Light, gorgeous yellow. He passed her one and took one of the same.

"What are these?" she wondered. Now, finally, she wanted to know.

"They're bliss." He smiled at her through his tears. "They're goggles that let you see the inner workings of the machine."

Sarah tugged at the lines of moss that ran between the old, crumbly cement tiles. Coarse strips of it. "Can I have another?" If she had two, then he would also.

He smiled. "Of course."

Sarah watched as he placed not one but two more tablets into his mouth, crunching them between his teeth, welcoming the effect to come on faster. And he was watching her. He was always watching her. So Sarah put them into her mouth. She looked away and stuck the dry tablets on the roof of her mouth. Felt the saliva pool in the bottom of her jaw, in front of her teeth.

Not too long ago, another night, she would have taken the tablets and they would have fallen into shared fantasies. Cuddled and whispered things. Sarah would have slept, like she longed to do nearly all of the time these days. Sleep and sleep, cocooned away. Kemp slumped back, head to the roof, and the tablets dissolved in her mouth. A bitter sludge. Do not swallow, she told herself. Do not take any in.

He turned his head and looked at her. His eyelids were heavy, weighted curtains. His smile was rubbery and slow.

"There isn't anyone else you do this kind of thing with. I'm the only one. I'm the only one who loves your everything."

Was that true? That couldn't be true. Because if *this* was who she was, then what was she worth? Certainly not love. She shook her head.

"Say something," he said.

She couldn't. Her mouth was full; she couldn't say *any-thing*. But Kemp's face began to crumple. He would howl. Another broken squelch of pain. So she leaned over him and kissed his lips. Cold and dry. She passed the slurry of spit and drugs from her mouth into his. He burbled and coughed and swallowed.

"Whoa," he said.

She wiped her mouth and looked away. Kemp kept on swallowing. He looked up at the lightening sky and swallowed all of her tablets and all of his. Was that too many? How many had he had in total? Five? Six? Seven? What had he taken before she'd gotten there? Was that danger-ous? What *were* those things? She reasoned her way out of it. He was a seasoned drug user. He would sleep this off.

"Oh my God, you're too much," he said. She took the baggie of remaining tablets from his hand. He held on, lightly, but she tugged it free. She shoved it deep into her pocket. She didn't want him to take any more. She didn't want him to hurt himself.

Soon, he was fast asleep, dead to the world. And while he breathed, heavy and slow, Sarah slipped away, down the laurel tree, almost falling when her hand gripped a loose shingle at the edge of the roof and pulled it free, spitting out over and over again the bitter taste.

31

Ali

Ali was exhausted. She made her coffee and her rice cake with peanut butter—look, healthy!—and sat at the kitchen table while Roommate One and Roommate Two buzzed about in big, soft pajamas, pink and fuzzy, already drinking champagne, already too loud. Ali looked at them. Two people she'd found on Craigslist. Strangers who considered her their friend.

"It's my bachelorette party!" Roommate One squealed.

"Get it!" Roommate Two said. "Something to be thankful for!"

They hadn't always been Roommate One and Roommate Two. Of course, when she'd first found them, she thought they were like her. Dirtbags looking for fun, and fuck the patriarchy. Follow our art no matter what. A musician, a writer. But it turned out the patriarchy had some pretty great Kool-Aid.

Ali wouldn't know. Kemp hadn't exactly tempted her; Adam neither. None of them had. The boys. The men. She concluded that her life might be better spent on her art and some light fucking on the side with whoever happened to be dancing with her when the last song played. Both her roommates now had careers and weddings on the horizon.

On the day Kemp had twisted her knee at the bus shelter and scared the shit out of her, she'd called her sisters afterward and told them everything about everything. Starting with Adam in the window.

"You fucking put on a show?" they said.

"You better start carrying some mace," they said.

"We're gonna send up our cousins to teach him a lesson," they said.

"Oh, I'm so sorry. That sounds really, really hard," they said. "You didn't deserve that."

And she breathed out, long and slow, what she hadn't realized she'd been holding for so long.

"Are you sure you want to go into work today?" Roommate One asked. "This is going to be *so* fun. Play hooky!"

"Oh, I wish I could," Ali said. "But because of the camping trip, I've already missed a day this week, and I'm missing tomorrow, so . . ."

Her roommates looked at her. Ali could almost see their thoughts. The camping trip. Whatever *that* was.

What you need to ask yourself, her sisters had told Ali on their phone call, *is what were you getting out of all that shit? You don't want to get yourself messed up in it again.*

Ali had just needed to get away. Roommates getting more basic by the day, Adam acting all weird, Sarah mean-eyeing her, and Kemp stalking her, twisting her knee. Away, away. Why hadn't she gone camping before? Because she was scared? Because she needed to wait for a man to take her? No, who needed them? She'd go. She'd go and get inspired. Isn't that what the outdoors did? Who cared if the gear was a little dirty? She was going camping after all. She was going *for the dirt*.

She bounced down back roads, south of Hood River, not to Lost Lake (where one night cost you forty dollars, she was horrified to find. Who paid forty dollars to camp?), but to a place an ex-almost-boyfriend, almost-best-friend she never saw anymore had shown her on a hike. A dimple of lake on the side of Mount Hood she didn't even know the name of. Think green trees, the night a crisp buffet on black water. Think the sway of Kemp's weed that she'd found, heady and green, in a shallow sandwich bag under a book on her bedside table. Think half-cooked rice and a can of over-salty chili. Think a whirling sensation at every crack and whoosh in the night. Was it Kemp? Finding her even out here? It was stupid to seek solitude. That's exactly where a sociopath would want you to be (watch scary movies much?), or at least a bear bingeing for his long winter's nap. Think mosquitoes, though it should have been too late in the season. Think global warming. Think minutes, unbearable minutes, passing like days. Think shivering the whole night through and waking up feeling like you've been hit by a truck, unable to get warm. Soon it would be Thanksgiving. What had she been thinking? How did anyone stand themselves, alone, for any stretch of time? No service out there. The sky was abuzz with celestial bodies but none would talk to the likes of her.

"I'll see you guys at the party," Ali said.

"Ohh," Roommate One pouted. "No fun."

"Tonight, after work," Ali said. "I'm really excited, but I can't, you know, piss off the boss anymore. I'm leaving *straight* from work. I really can't wait."

A winery. A gaggle of goosenecked women all bloomed pale and dewy from the same genus of plant. A necklace of dicks. But tasteful. Lots of pink. So much pink in so many shades. Was it because of pussy? The symbolism of letting the girls' most valuable treasure go? Did someone order a stripper? No, but second best, we're all getting pole dancing lessons! Would the men be doing the same? Would they be practicing how to sexually satisfy their partners? Would they be modeling underwear for each other?

"Love you, babe!" Said Roommate One or Two. Ali's back was to them, and she found that, actually, they sounded exactly the same. Perhaps they *were* the same. But literally. Was she in a horror movie where the slow realization came to our hero that she was the lone person in a sea of clones? She'd tell this thought to her sisters. Oh, how they would laugh. She was at the door, a prickle on her neck. In fact, Ali couldn't remember which one's party was this weekend. One or Two? The events were only three weeks apart. But it didn't really matter, did it? She smiled to herself.

As Ali went to her car, 9:15 in the morning, already a little late, she heard something, an argument, around the corner of Adam's house. She walked past her car and peered down the driveway. Sam, the homeless man who fished their street for cans, was standing before Sarah, feet planted, telling her off. Sarah was in a thin shirt that was almost see-through. She had wild, sleep-mussed hair, and her eyeballs were pinwheeling. She looked deranged. Ali threaded her keys between her knuckles and stepped into the street.

"I know you hide them away!" Sam said. "I know there's more than just some Jif jars."

Sarah was next to the blue recycling bin, with newspapers and plastic cases that used to hold baby tomatoes and baby spinach—infant vegetables—and cardboard boxes strewn at her feet.

"I do not," Sarah said. Then she noticed Ali, and a rush of relief flashed across her face. "Hey!"

"Sam," Ali said, putting her hand behind her back. "What are you going on about now?"

Sam looked at her, and for a second there was nothing behind those pale, blue eyes. Then after an emerging realization, he took a long, shuddery breath. "Hi, Ali," he said.

"Sam, why are you yelling?"

"I just . . ." he shuffled his feet. He liked Ali, and what had it cost her? Bagging up their recycling for him. Giving him leftovers now and again. It wasn't that hard. Being kind to people who didn't have what they needed. "She hides away my cans."

"Sam, I'm headed to a bachelorette party this weekend," Ali said. She had once tried to give him money, but he'd pushed her tight wad of thirteen dollars away, insisting that he *needed* to work for it. "Tonight, actually. You *know* we're gonna be drinking there. I was thinking I could bring back the cans for you. If you wanted."

"Yeah, OK," Sam said, a different creature now. "Thank you, thank you."

After he left, Ali and Sarah stood in silence. Sarah hated her, and if the roles were reversed, Ali would hate her too. And she didn't even know why she had done the things she'd done in that window. She couldn't coherently answer the question her sisters had asked. What had she gotten out of it? It was just . . . It hadn't been about Adam. It hadn't been about Sarah. It had been about exerting a little control in a life that bored her and seemed to be drifting. Portland a let-down. Less hippie magic, more Patagonia tech-money fleece.

So, on those nights, to fuck with Adam. To control him. The epitome of Portland. Pour-over coffee and Patagonia fleeces. It scratched something.

Sarah was shaking, but she seemed to be coming-to from some kind of waning spell.

"Thank you," she said. "I'm home sick, and I thought I heard someone in my house and . . ."

"In your house?"

"It must have been a bad dream. Then I came out here, and Sam was dumping out the recycling."

"Here, let me help you," Ali said.

Together, they stooped to the work of putting the recycling back into the can.

"Sorry," Sarah said. Her voice was high and thin, a ribbon that could decorate a present but not carry weight. "Sam hates me because I don't like his politics and . . ."

Ali studied her. "Wait, you really *do* hide the cans?"

Sarah's face flushed red, then she laughed. "It's embarrassing."

"Sam's basically a good guy," Ali said. "Basically. He's just . . . He didn't mean anything by it. He just has these lines he says because he thinks he's supposed to say them."

"Yeah, I guess you're right."

"Listen," Ali said. "I feel like I should have said *I'm* sorry. You know. A long time ago."

"Thanks," Sarah said. She was laughing, wiping tears out of her eyes. "I feel like I should have said fuck you a long time ago."

Ali laughed. "I *might* have deserved that. I don't know what I was thinking."

"I don't know what *I* was thinking," Sarah said. "We're all fucking up. All the time. Adam should never have . . . We weren't doing well and he put that on you and that wasn't fair either. It doesn't matter. We're even."

"We're what?" Ali said.

"I mean, we'll just have to be better."

"Yeah, or maybe I just move back home," Ali said. "Get out of the fucking rain."

And Sarah hooted out a laugh, big and ugly, too much in that early morning by far. Ali had the impression that she was showing her something she shouldn't be allowed to see. Was she drunk?

"No, I'm serious," she said, and in the way some decisions can be, she realized as she said it that she was. "I'm getting the fuck out."

*   *   *

When Ali got to work, Candice showed her the box full of drugs. And poison, maybe? That's what Candice thought, and Ali had to admit, it did look bad. What the actual fuck? It was like something the detectives on *CSI* would find in a rich white kid's boarding-school locker. Ali looked up. People in suits and skirts kept coming into the lobby. A never-ending supply. Some of them jammed umbrellas into boxes on either side of the main entrance. Fuller and fuller. How many more could possibly fit? The only people in the entire city who seemed to use umbrellas all worked in this single building. Everyone else in Portland wore raincoats and considered umbrellas a scarlet letter implying your geographic promiscuity. Ali had made sure to never use one so that she could fit in. It was ridiculous. But these important, get-it-done people on their way to someplace big did not care.

"I knew you partied, girl, but damn!" Candice said. "Are you trying to kill someone?"

"No, of course not," Ali said.

"Poison!"

"No. I didn't order this."

"You don't text back, you don't call, hell, I even called that boy of yours."

This shook her.

"Crispin?"

"Not him," Candice said. "That neighbor boy you've got the hots for."

Adam. If Candice had called him, it made more sense why Adam had been worried, though it still didn't explain why he might climb the laurel and look into her window.

"I don't—" Ali reached into her scalp, itching her head. "I never had the hots for him."

"Peep show every night!"

"I wish you hadn't called him."

"I was worried about you!"

"Did he . . . What did he sound like?"

"You mean, was he sweating you?" Candice held it there, just a moment, brought back to her old self. "Was he worried about you? Did he want to be your knight in shining armor? Was he thinking with his sword? Is that what you want to know?"

"No, that's not what I meant."

"Well, he was."

"He was?"

Candice laughed. "Girl, you know he was. He wants to scoop you up. I could almost hear the erection over the phone. Towers getting interference."

Ali tapped the desk. She hadn't even taken off her coat.

"I was fine," she said. "I went camping. I got a new job from Mel Sweetney. She liked those T-shirts I did for that school."

"Kemp's mom's school," Candice said.

"I was looking for inspiration."

"But camping?"

"Yeah, I can go camping."

"Congrats about the job, really, I'm proud of you, but usually people call in about that," Candice said, a little sullen. "Usually they're letting their coworkers know before they drive out to God-knows-where so at least they can cover for them. No cell phone service. You might have gotten eaten by a bear! Did you know you might have been eaten by a bear?"

A bear? Didn't Candice realize there were so many things with sharper teeth than bears? Like Kemps. Mother and son. She looked at the box and saw the Logicstyx sticker.

"Shit." Ali pushed the box away. "What the fuck is going on?"

"Right?" Candice said.

"But why would Kemp have been so dumb to leave a Logicstyx sticker on it?"

"Maybe he wants you to know it was him so then—"

"I don't care, I'm not going to try and think in his circles."

"You sure you didn't . . . ?"

"I'm not buying drugs," Ali said. "At least, not fucking poison! Come on, Candice."

It didn't matter. She was done. She was absolutely done with the whole Kemp family. On the way to work, she'd dropped the T-shirts off for Evie and found her agitated, pacing her office. True, Kemp had gotten her the job, and true, it had led to the work with Mel, but still, Ali didn't think she had to be so dismissive.

Ali looked up, a box of the shirts in her hands, each one carefully screen-printed, and saw a slippery little fish-tail moment that was so fast she wasn't totally sure it happened. Disgust. Evie was disgusted by her.

Ali unfolded the top shirt and held it up. Evie had wanted the shirts to be cool. To be something the teachers would actually want to wear. In the end, they settled on a simple and blocky design. The text echoed backward like a cheap video effect from twenty years ago.

The shirt read, *We see everyone at CES.*

Ali thought it had turned out well, but when she asked about next year's shirts, Evie said, *We're going in another direction* as if she was saying *Fuck you*. Then Evie watched Ali bring in box after box after box, sweating and getting later and later for her job by the minute, never once offering to help.

When all the boxes had been deposited in Evie's clean, white office, Evie scribbled out a check covering the remainder of Ali's fee and looked at her with a little smile held in her teeth.

I'm sorry my son broke up with you, but you must have realized, it was never about you at all.

Listen, Ali had said. *I broke up with him.*

Now, Ali stared at the box of drugs in her hands.

"What are we gonna do with it?" Candice asked.

"Throw it away," Ali said.

"Yeah, that's what Adam said you should do too."

That was it. Ali took the box and marched out of the lobby, the bright ghosts of the high fluorescent lights following her steps, the men and women in their dark clothing, all in a rush. All around the country, in the bigger cities, the nodes of real financial flex, people were doing the same. Let's move that money. Up the ladder, up the ladder. Move that money up the ladder! And Kemp and his mother were up there, sitting on their rungs, peering down and seeing if their loogies would hit people like her.

Out through the big, revolving doors into the hush of bad weather, or rather, just weather, because it would be the same, not better or worse, for the next three or four months straight. Raindrops loud on cardboard. Tap, tap, tap, the Logicstyx sticker peeling up. She was a woman in possession of a small pharmacy of controlled substances. He'd taken it way too far.

She stuffed the box as deep as the overflowing trash can would allow and hated every passerby watching her, wondering. Soft, caring liberals warrioring for the planet and social justice and wearing Nikes and driving Jeeps. And fuck them, this was the kind of shit that was in all their hearts.

PART 4
Like a House On Fire

Getting away from this rainy ass place

Mark your calendars. I'm coming home.

POSTED BY UNKNOWN AT 3:07 AM
1 COMMENTS:

Crispin said:

Do you want to know why I did this? I did it because of you.

32

Adam

IT HAD BEEN no more than three or four minutes, five at
the most. It felt longer, though, before the sirens came.
By then, the smoke was a huge black snake, rising up to the
promise of wind. The fire probably had been working far
longer than Adam knew. Small tongues softened up the
mealy guts of that rotting house. There were fire trucks, two
of them, and more on the way judging by sirens exploding
down César Chávez Boulevard. It was a dark, heavy November day, but the fire was brighter than anything the sun could
manage. Flames danced on the roof, scorching the air. Adam
would be able to call it up behind his eyes for the rest of his
life. He'd recall it any time he needed to remember the kind
of material he was actually made of and what he was willing
to do for love of family. Those aching flames and that squealing ruckus descended upon his block. Like a house on fire.
Why did people say that? *The roof, the roof, the roof is on fire.*
Adam certainly didn't need any water. Let the motherfucker
burn. He'd never seen anything like it before, at least not

outside the movies. But there it was: Ali's house going up. And it was beautiful.

What did he do, did he do something, what did he do, did he do something, what did he do? He did something.

Adam wasn't a killer. Despite all of the fixations, the intrusive thoughts, the violent tableaus that had come to him over the years, he'd never actually *do* anything. He *had* thought about it, really considered whether there was any circumstance in which he might be able to end someone's life. He even imagined himself into moments where Sarah and Maddie were about to be killed and to save them all he had to do was . . . and realized he couldn't do it. So what did that say about him? What kind of man did that make him?

But he could light a match.

It was the shingle and it was the crows. After he'd seen Evie, after he'd gone to the duck pond, he put it all together. There had been a shingle in the laurel because Ali's window had only been the start of Crispin Kemp's climb. He had gone all the way to the roof, and he hadn't been alone. Though now he was. The crows tipped Adam him off to that. The crows and their wheeling pleads, gathering atop Ali's house. Crows would eat anything. Whenever Tina caught a rat in one of her basement traps, she would toss the little gray body into the street and those black birds made quick, loud work of it. Maddie babbled and pointed at the water, at the sky, at every trash can they passed. Everything was here and everything was amazing, and he took out his phone and looked at the photo of the crows. He realized it wasn't the same as those times he'd seen them along the waterfront, perching on every available branch, flustered and chaotic. These birds were focused. They were attendants to a feast.

There was someone dead on the roof.

So, a deposit into his bankrupt heart, it was Sarah who had done it. It was Sarah who had proven she was willing to do *anything* for Adam. He thought of her then, upstairs sleeping, traumatized, he was sure. PTSD. They didn't have much time. He spent the day pacing the living room, wondering what he could do. Because how do you show love to someone with dirt on their hands? And then he had it.

You get yourself dirty too.

* * *

Adam wondered who had called the fire department. He hadn't. He hadn't even been sure if the fire would take. He was new to arson. But here it was, blooming, curing, saving. The heat was intense. A physical presence that seemed to meander, like the fire was bored with its work, underwhelmed at the low-caloric fuel of that junky house, hungry for more. More. More. It ached toward the houses on either side, and they flirted back, smoke beginning to appear on their roofs. Mrs. Jenkins was out, thank God, standing with her cat in her arms. A small shelf of flame appeared in the boughs of the pine tree in Ali's backyard. Adam watched a family of squirrels hustle down, scrambling wide-stanced, nose-first. It was an adult squirrel with three babies, the last of which had orange flames dancing on the tip of its tail. Then they were gone behind the veil of smoke.

"Oh, shit!" Adam said. He was excited; he was devastated. His nervous system had tapped into a power source too much for his body. This thing should be felt by an elephant. By a mastodon. A brontosaurus. No way he was up for it. He'd overdose. He tried to feel nothing. He tried. He thought of the things he'd been taught in grade school. Stop, drop, and roll. Get down, below the smoke. Firemen may look like monsters, but they were there to help. "Oh, shit!"

For some reason, the firefighters seemed to be spraying only in one window, Ali's window, a concentrated spray unequal to the task. Adam took out his phone and googled it. The top answer was that there might be someone inside. Something called a NIST strategy. The spray could push the smoke and flames, domino temperatures inside the house, increase the possibility of survivors. A full-on deluge might cause the structure to collapse, reducing the likelihood of survival, so first the firefighters needed to be sure. *Was* there someone inside? A cold, trickling fear crept up his left side. He had been sure there was nobody inside. He had been *absolutely* sure. It was Friday. Ali and the rest had left for the bachelorette party yesterday.

Did he do something, what did he do, did he . . .

Adam watched from the porch with Maddie in his arms. He expected to see other creatures descend from the tree and admit themselves to Salmon Street in broad daylight—raccoons, owls, opossums—as if the contract between the nocturnal and diurnal worlds was suspended, obviously, due to an act of God, but none did. He thought of the poor squirrel with its tail alight. Perhaps it had enough sense to belly into the pool Ali and her roommates had abandoned in the backyard. Perhaps it had put itself out.

Maddie was entranced by the flames. Another wonder of the world! Everything, to her, was as it should be because she was too young to know better. Houses sometimes burst into flames! *Very* interesting. Colorful and hot. Adam was proud. Most kids her age would be terrified, he was sure.

"Do you see it burning?" He cooed to her. "Crackle, crackle, crackle."

There was nobody in that house. The firemen were just being careful. He tried to think of a song about fire. A nursery rhyme. He couldn't think of anything. So, he settled on singing her "Ring Around the Rosie," but at the end, he changed it to *It all burns down.*

What must he look like, singing to his daughter about a house on fire? But people wouldn't hear what he was singing. They would just see a father soothing a child. And Maddie loved the song. She kept giggling and patting her tiny, chubby hands together. He didn't need to read any baby books! In fact, he could probably write one. He'd call it *Benign Neglect.* The *Tiger Mom* for white dudes.

But this was bad! he reminded himself. *It would go, it would burn, it would go, it would burn, it would go, it would . . .*

In fact, the heat was a little uncomfortable now. How strange that so much potential for destruction was stored up in that small house: bad foundation, cracks in the floorboards, windows crooked in their casings. But, he supposed it was like a neutron bomb or something—lots of damage laid up in a small device if only you got the reactions right.

He took a picture with his phone. He was always taking pictures with his phone. You're getting this? Oh, shit, yes, I'm getting this. Anyone would. In fact, *everyone* was. All up and down the block, his neighbors were snapping photos.

"You should go inside," a fireman called to him. "It's not good to be out here with the smoke and everything.

Especially for her." He motioned to Maddie. "In fact, if you have any other place you could go, just for the day, until this is taken care of, that might be for the best."

"OK," Adam said. He was ashamed to be holding a baby. Both for the potential harm that could befall Maddie from the smoke and chemicals stirred up in the conflagration, but also because, before this man in his suit and hat, fit and brave with an unimpeachable job (nobody ever said fuck the firemen) he felt like a loser. But he wasn't a loser, was he? This was all because of him. This was all because he refused to lose his family.

"There are three women who live there," Adam said.

"What was that?" The fireman was already turning back to the flames, which they were *still* only spraying in the one window. Most of their hoses, instead, were focused on the houses on either side, preventing them from being taken too.

"There are three women who live there," Adam said again. "They're our neighbors, so I thought you should know."

"OK," the fireman said. "Thank you. Are you aware if any of them were home?"

"I—" Adam thought of Ali and her roommates, off at some rented home high on a hill in wine country. "I don't really know. I was up pretty late with this one." He jiggled Maddie about until he shook free a chortle. The fireman didn't seem to notice how cute she was. Why did anyone else bother having kids when he obviously had the best one? "But no pets. At least not any I know of." Had he asked about pets? Did anyone care about pets? *What did he do, did he do something?*

"OK, thank you."

"Are you going to put it out?"

"Sir," the fireman said sternly. "Our first priority is the rescue of lives."

Maddie began crying and Adam shifted her from one hip to the other, worried, absurdly (at least he recognized it!), that the motion came across as feminine. She was radiating heat from her diaper. Foul things awaited his attention.

"Let me know if you need any help."

"Right," the fireman said. "I'll do that."

*   *   *

The fire was the day's entertainment. He texted Sarah, who after having spent most of yesterday sleeping, was back at school, saying she felt refreshed. That morning, before she left, she smiled at him, a little embarrassed by what they had done last night, and said TGIF. He sent her photos and assured her that he could not smell too much smoke in the house and, yes, the windows were all closed tightly, Maddie was safe.

i just hope everyone's ok, she texted.

Firemen said everyone out of house.
Bachelorette party, remember?

. . .

It must have started right after you
left for work.

I thought I smelled something.

At least that old place will be gone.
New construction. New beginning.

Prob some ugly skinny homes

How are you feeling?
>
> Fine!
>
> Or, good as can be expected

Then Adam watched her three agitated dots, signaling that she was composing something either lengthy or which required a lot of tact and thought. In the end, nothing came, and it was probably because she had been pulled away to teach or because the principal, Kemp's mother (everyone had a mother), had summoned her to her office for a heart to heart before the weekend started. Maybe she would ask about the smoothie she had left, the crows, or how messy their house was. Or maybe Sarah had stopped texting back simply because she was angry he'd known about the bachelorette party at all. There were no moon-shots. You gathered altitude a little at a time.

But was he feeling fine? Hard to be sure. And he didn't have to be! So long as he kept going.

He texted Ali.

> Are you ok?

What??

> Was there a lot of yr art in there?

Why are you asking? You can't
talk to me anymore, remember?

Was that the deal? Maybe it was one of those things everyone knew implicitly. Leave a penny, lower your brights on a dark highway, say *I'm busy, I'm busy* when the Save the Children people tried to corner you in their red vests. Don't talk to the peep show across the street after you've been caught. Still, this was thrilling, wasn't it? How often did you see something like *this*?

sorry, just wanted to check.

Your watching my life burn down.

sorry

Stop texting me. Stop saying sorry.

33

Evie

IT WAS EARLY, six in the morning, Monday, and I was scanning in with my badge at the front door of the school. My hands were full—purse, Starbucks cup, gym bag—and the scanner wasn't taking my credentials. The school chickens watched me from their wired-in run, clucking. *Bleh!* The scanner scolded me. *Bleh!* I swear the chickens *smiled* at me. Nervous bitches. The harem of old heads, not an egg among them. The scanner yelled at me again, red light flashing. *Bleh!*

"Hello, Mrs. Kemp?"

I turned, and there you were, a small, trim Asian woman standing on the path behind me. You had the look of a professional swinging by on your way to the office. Smart blue jeans, so dark they might be black, cream-colored blouse, and a suit jacket, dark blue again. You had a rich voice, something for radio. Bigger than your body. You couldn't have been more than thirty-five. I thought you were the parent of a prospective student. Here I was, the gatekeeper, and *you* were trying to get in. And why not. Chávez Elementary is a jewel in the PPS system. Overeager parents are always conniving ways to run into me, make an impression, increase the chances their kids will be admitted. Never mind it's a randomized lottery. Nobody believes it's truly left to chance.

"If you'll call the main office," I said, bending to set my coffee on the ground, "they can give you some information."

"Here, let me," you said. You came forward easily, a spring released. You held out your hand for the cup, and I gave it to you. Quad-shot venti nonfat latte. The language we have. All nonsense. Our fingers touched, briefly, just along the top of my forefinger, the bottom of your pinky. Soft hands. Can we know anything from the random intimacies we share? I believed right then that I could trust you.

Then, once I was free of the coffee, I managed to hold my badge to the scanner true, a clean slap—*boop!*—a green light, the latch springing free. I turned and pressed the bar with my butt and took back the coffee. It wasn't the normal Evie Kemp show, I'll admit. Usually, I took pains to always present ease. But this was too early. This was supposed to be behind the scenes.

"Like I said, just call the main office during normal hours, and Sandra can set you up with a tour. And, of course, if you'd like to meet some of the teachers, we have informational meetings in the spring. Most parents find them *very* helpful." I was being kind but also taking care to cut with my voice. The effect would be, I hoped, that you would get the message but never be able to say I was anything but courteous.

"No, Mrs. Kemp, my name is Detective Lumen. I'm not . . . This isn't about enrollment. I'm wondering if I could ask you a few questions?"

"OK." A detective. I thought maybe it was to do with a student in my school. An abusive situation perhaps, the midnight call. That would explain why you were here so early. Privacy, a heads-up. It's happened a few times in my career. The terrible things our children suffer.

"It's about your son," you said. "Crispin?"

His name from your lips. How off-putting. A minor chord. And there, just then, a belief inside me, battered over the years but still held with enforced rigging, began to animate under fresh wind. Had he done something? What had he done?

Just the Thursday before, Ali had delivered the T-shirts. I had behaved in a regrettable way. She had done nothing wrong, after all. I wondered if perhaps she had told Crispin about it. Perhaps he'd acted out. I had the urge to call my husband.

"Why? Is there something wrong?" I swallowed an angular lump. There was snot back there. Maybe I was coming down with a cold in the last stretch before the Thanksgiving holidays.

The winds picked up. The belief yearned against its anchors. If my son, my special son, had done . . . I knew my belief would fly away forever.

"Can we speak someplace private?" you wondered, and I appreciated the caution in your voice. You didn't have to do that. You have such empathy. "In your office, perhaps?"

I felt myself drifting backward, against the door, pressing it open. My hands trembled. The air was cold, wasn't it a little too cold? The chickens, with their little black eyes, were all watching. I wished they would get to their scrabbling business. I would pluck the lot and put them in a stew.

"I, uh . . ." I took a drink of my coffee. A mouthful of foam. There was nothing in foam. I tipped the cup to a higher angle. The fast, hot tongue of the coffee reached my mouth. I was Evie Kemp. I *handled* situations, every kind, even this one. "I really don't think now is the best time for whatever it is that Crispin has gotten himself involved in. Perhaps we could arrange for a time for me to come down? I can take your card and meet you at the station. I have a busy day. Mondays are always so chaotic."

"Mrs. Kemp," you said, and I began to hate the care that had entered your voice. "Your son was involved in an accident. He's . . ."

"Don't," I said. The air was bright. Crisp. Breathe in too quickly and it might cut for tears. It didn't matter, my eyes were already welling. Before, when Crispin was being questioned by the police for his little prank on Tamara, it had come with an aura of lightness. I could still believe he was just a heartbroken boy going a little above and beyond with his kiss-off. So what? He sent drugs to his ex's place of work. So he wanted to cause her some trouble. It wasn't good. I knew it wasn't normal or acceptable, but you could at least *understand* it. But if he had gone even further, oh God, if he had *hurt* someone . . .

"Not here," I said. Any teacher or front office person or, God forbid, a parent might arrive at any moment. "Inside. My office."

You nodded. You understood. Your face was blank, ready to display whatever was needed. You were good at this. I would have to be careful with you.

The automatic lights took a moment to activate, and so you followed me into the dark. Involved in an accident? What had Crispin done? Did he do something? The lights clicked to life at just the last moment before it became concerning. We went into the waiting area, then beyond, into my office. I set my things on the desk, started up the sound machine, an oceanic muffle, a trick I'd learned long ago to keep the things said and done in my office private. I sat down. I motioned for you to do the same.

"There was a fire," you said.

"I just want you to know," I told you. "Crispin has a good heart. He's very talented, exceptional really, he just sometimes gets carried away."

"I believe that," you said, wincing. "But there was a fire, and we think that your son died."

He was dead? He'd started a fire? No. Think. I had to think. There was an open variable in the equation. There had to be. Do the math right and Crispin wasn't dead. But you looked so sad. I remember that. I'll always remember how sad you looked.

Of course I had considered what it might be like to lose my child. Every parent does. That came with birth, all at once, of an instant. To be given something precious was also to wonder how long you were going to be allowed to keep it. Sometimes I would go out with Crispin in his little onesies, and I'd see other mothers and feel so sorry for them. *They* didn't have a baby like *I* did. Crispin looked like the picture on a jar of Gerber's. *You are so lucky,* I remember other moms telling me. *He's perfect.*

"I'm so sorry," you said. "I can't imagine your loss."

"Are you sure?" I wondered.

"When was the last time you saw your son?"

"I—I'll have to think." This seemed an odd question. Was Crispin really dead? Was *I* suspected of something?

"We had him over for dinner," I said. "A little more than a week ago."

"Was there anything off about that meeting? Anything that seemed outside of his normal character?"

He'd been upset. Ali had just broken up with him. Didn't speak all through the meal as Mike tried to pry from him information about Logicstyx. I hadn't thought anything of it. That was how they talked. Or not talked. Then, after dinner, Mike went off to minister to his cigars or his koi, and Crispin drove off, back out into the night, back out to her.

"So, eight or nine days ago?" you said, writing in a notebook. It must be terrible to tell someone news like this. Of course you wanted to do something with your hands. Write away and cover for your thoughts, your measuring. Were you looking at me and wondering what I was capable of? Were you questioning if I had something to do with my son's death?

"We usually see him more than that," I insisted, because we did, didn't we? Such a sweet boy. Troubled, but sweet. It was so important that you understood how much we loved him. "But he was in Seattle for the week. For work. We love him. We loved him very much."

"I am so sorry for your loss," you said.

"Are you sure?" I wondered. "Are you absolutely sure?"

"Do you know if he ever made it up to Seattle? We're working under the assumption that he stayed here in Portland."

I looked at you, opened my hands, began to say something to try and grab hold of this conversation.

But you went on. "You mentioned that his boss was calling you? That he hadn't been showing up to meetings?"

Had I said that? Honestly, I wasn't sure. I was saying things apart from my thinking. I was just talking, babbling on, like one of those fucking hens outside. Was I had out? But for what? I was wondering, *Are you trying to catch me?* I shifted in my chair.

"Are you . . . are you really sure?"

You nodded your head. "He left a concerning comment on Ali Washington's personal blog that seems to state an intent to self-harm, and we've found remains that match."

The belief in my heart shed its rigging, its tentative hold, but not to fly away and abandon me. Instead, it had found a new strength and it wrapped about my heart, succored to the smooth muscle, firm and tight. Too tight? It never can be. Not with certain kinds of love. He was so special.

"Crispin," I said.

"I'm so sorry I can't be more clear. That's what I'm trying to figure out. I hope I'm wrong. But I want to be honest with you."

A wave would come. I knew that. A wall of water would tumble upon me and take away my senses. I would be raked over submerged rocks, spat out bleeding, gasping, crying. A son. That's not something you were supposed to lose. A husband, a lifestyle, a fortune. All of those could be had again. But a son? *This son?* I hadn't taken his breakup with Ali or his fixation with Sarah seriously enough. And now I was paying. Something had happened, my son was dead, and something had happened to make it so, and you were trying to help. But I couldn't trust you.

"His cell phone has been identified as being in the house when it burned down. And."

"The house?" I said. "*His* house?"

"It's on Salmon Street. Not too far from here. Between 42nd and 43rd?"

"His girlfriend," I said.

"Right, that's what I was hoping to figure out. We're trying to nail down who saw him last, and we have a description, but it's—"

"Ali Washington," I said. If that woman had anything to do with my son dying . . . I looked at the T-shirts sitting in the boxes.

"I think I have a picture of her on my phone," I said. Of course I had pictures of Ali on my phone. I had a dozen pictures. After Crispin started seeing her, I endeavored to know everything I could about her. So I hired her to make the T-shirts. "I can give you a description, if that helps."

"Yes, we are in contact with Ali Washington, but that wasn't the woman described to us. I believe her and your son had broken up by the time of the fire. Your son was seen with someone else on Wednesday morning, only the witness isn't reliable."

"What?"

"A man said that Crispin was on the roof of the house, Ali Washington's house, with a black-haired woman, short, medium build. White. But he also said that she smelled like peanut butter. He . . . he says her name is Peanut Butter Cunt, which obviously isn't helpful, but I can't help but think there might be *something* to it."

"Fuck."

"The witness deals with some mental health issues," Detective Lumen admitted. "What I wondered was if you knew if Crispin had begun dating someone new. I know he and Ali only recently broke up, but you never know. With apps these days, people move on quickly. I just had to check it out, and I understand that you and your son were *very* close. If anyone would know—"

"Fuck!" I said, but the word didn't hold any of the anger I had meant it to. It was flimsy, cut-rate. "Sarah Cooper."

You nodded your head. "I'll go as slow as you need me to. But this here is the hard part." You handed me a packet of tissues. "I'm going to ask you a lot of questions, and it's absolutely critical that right now you tell me everything you know. That you answer every single question with complete honesty, even if you think it makes you sound bad, or casts you or your family in a bad light. *This* is how we'll get to the bottom of it. Because my number one job here is to get to the bottom of it."

I looked into your eyes and I wondered what that might look like. Spilling my whole story, absolutely no lies, just the entire, ugly truth. It wouldn't come all at once. I wasn't going to give it to you all at once. But what would it feel like to be picked at? To have your thumbnail find the seam in my shell? To have you open me up completely and tell you everything. To tell you how my son had always had . . . issues, how he lashed out, how he couldn't take no for an answer, and how he skulked around the edges. How my husband found security footage of him jerking off on our car. How, recently, he'd been getting worse. How, sometimes, he scared me.

"OK," I said.

"OK," you said, and you seemed encouraged. You sat a little bit straighter. "Let's start at the beginning. Can you tell me what kind of person your son was?"

"Sure." I took a deep breath.

But I could never do it. Give everything away like that. After all, it is what you keep from people that gives you power. Anybody who doesn't know that, doesn't have power. And so, I lied.

"Crispin was just a normal young man," I said. "He had his troubles, like everyone does, but he was a sweet boy, and I loved him."

CHAPTER

34

Sarah

THE DETECTIVES SHOWED up at her classroom door,
wondering if she had a moment to talk. Really, of
course, she didn't. It was the last week before conferences,
and she had a million things to do. Kids tugged at her leg.
Someone was complaining about a missing Tech Deck,
and Luke had taken it in his mind to piece together multiple student's projects in a grand, complete exhibit of the
salmon life cycle—not a bad idea, actually. In fact, when
Sarah saw it together like that, a realization came to her,
whole and holy. Sometimes, like salmon spawning, life
demanded death. It was Monday, it was hectic, there were
a million fires to put out.

"It'll take just a few minutes," Detective Lumen said.
"I believe you have a break coming up?"

Sarah did, in fact, have a break coming up. And they
did, in fact, already know this. Fear, curiously, seemed
to grow inside her tongue and nowhere else. A lingually
contained infection. It was inflaming. She was thinking

clearly, and her armpits remained breezy, but her tongue thickened.

She swallowed and managed to say, "Of course."

She was due to drop her class off at the library in three minutes, and then she would be prepping materials for the math lesson. Twenty-eight baggies holding exactly nineteen cents each. Well, the math lesson could be thrown to GoNoodle. It would have to be. She wasn't under the impression that she could say no to these people. Didn't want to. Wouldn't that look suspicious? So she sent the class away with the para, Ted, who gave her a look of terror as he headed out at the head of her class (a mistake already), and the kids at the end of the line mustered to take as much advantage as they could.

"I don't have *all that* much time," Sarah insisted. "My prep is now and then it's down to the pumping room. Output my daily quota, you know?"

"Quota?" the male detective, Prichard, wondered.

"She's pumping breast milk," Detective Lumen said. "For her baby? At home?"

"Right—" Prichard nodded vigorously. He seemed like the kind of man who pretended women didn't shit, or vomit, or produce milk from their breasts. He smelled like wool. His overcoat was huge but he was even bigger. Sarah doubted he could manage to button it to the top anymore. She suspected if she asked him about high school, he'd have a story about the best years of his life. What a guy.

The detectives sat down in two small, blue plastic seats and motioned that she should sit as well. Prichard almost pulled it off, except his trousers rucked up high enough to expose his pale, blotchy shin skin. Lumen had no problem at all. She looked like she routinely sat in too-small chairs and, in fact, might prefer it. Sarah sat in her own chair, a little flustered now. She had years of experience watching parents squeeze into their student's desks. The awkwardness, the fumble and giggle as they lowered themselves, had always worked to release tension. Let's share a laugh. And, wow, she thought, these detectives had already claimed this space, her time, as their own as if she were the visitor and they were the hosts. She began to sweat.

"We're wondering about the fire," Detective Lumen said. "We have a few questions."

"Do they . . . ?" Sarah caught herself. She felt like there was too much in her mouth. She had to be careful, speak clearly. She closed her eyes and visualized her tongue tap-dancing out the words. "You talked with my husband, and he was under the impression . . ." She opened her eyes and looked from one detective to the other. "Do *you* think it was set on purpose?"

"Yes," Detective Prichard said. "It is looking that way. What we might be looking at is a suicide."

"But all the girls were out," Sarah said. "We were told they were all out of town."

"Yes, all the women are safe," Detective Lumen said. "The victim wasn't any of them."

"We think it might be Ali Washington's boyfriend," Detective Prichard said. "Or, ex-boyfriend. We think it might be a message. He was trying to send a message."

"Jesus, shut up," Lumen said, just to him. "That's not for sure."

Prichard looked down into his meaty hands. This might be an act, Sarah considered. All the detectives in TV shows and books had one. The blubbered overshare, the feigned schism. They were hunting for something from her. A reaction. A tell. What had Evie Kemp told them? What did Evie Kemp know? Sarah felt overmatched. She was tired.

"That's . . . that's some message," Sarah said in almost a whisper.

"What did you say?" Lumen asked.

"I said, if that's what it was, then it was a *hell* of a message."

"You're telling me," Prichard said.

"He was—" Detective Lumen leaned forward, her hands folded loosely between her knees, a gesture meant to show she was blocking Prichard from the conversation. This is just the two of us girls. You're safe. "We've spoken to Ali and, as we understand it, he was very distraught. He seemed, in the last few days, to be unable to accept that their relationship had ended. He was acting strange. Aggressive. Sent her a suspicious package. And it looks like he was last seen on her roof. A witness saw him on the roof, where the fire was started. And he left a message in the comments of her blog."

"He was seen on the roof? How?" They had a witness? Her glands rallied to produce all the chemicals. Fight or flight? Who had seen him on the roof? Was it Sam? Had he spotted her after all? The light from Tina's. It had blinded them. She thought she had leaned back in time, away from view. Had Sam really seen her and Kemp together? Or were they fishing?

"But aren't those roofs, like, fire resistant?" She directed this question to Prichard. She wanted to call him back into the conversation. She liked her odds with him better. "They call them cement shingles. Are they really made of cement? How can cement burn? Cement can't burn, can it?"

"I don't know," Prichard said thoughtfully. "You know, I don't think they can, actually."

"Well," Lumen said, "he was covered in accelerant, wasn't he?"

"Yeah, true," Prichard said. "Rather extreme, really. To go like that. But, I guess if you put gasoline on anything, it's gonna burn."

"Gasoline?" Sarah said.

"It's a pretty hard way to go," Lumen said, eyes locked on Sarah. "To light yourself on fire. There's a lot of steps there. There's a lot of time to reconsider."

"Are you saying . . . ?"

Prichard edged in. "What I'm wondering is if he seemed like the kind of guy who'd go through all of that and still light the match."

"We're wondering," Lumen said. "Because, and I know this doesn't always carry water, but it looked like things were going pretty well for him from the outside. His company was due to go public very soon. He was going to make *a lot* of money."

"Well, I know Ali just broke up with him," Sarah said.

"Oh yeah?" Lumen said. "Was that a pretty big deal? Was he pretty into her?"

"Do you know what that's like, Sarah?" Prichard said, waiting for her to look back up from the floor so he could catch her eyes. "Do you know what it's like to have someone really *sweating* you?"

That last night on the roof, she had left Kemp while he was asleep. How many tablets did he take? Three. And what even were they? Ecstasy? Special K? OxyContin? Some combination? She hadn't known. Stupid. She'd just wanted him to be quiet. To leave her alone. She'd kissed in two more. So five total? Six? Seven? Did that make her a killer? Would they find her DNA on his lips? No, the fire. The fire must have burned that all away. But Kemp was sleeping. And the days didn't add up. Two days later and *then* the fire starts. So *who* started the fire? Divine luck? Some invisible force out there, helping her? But fuck, she'd moved his truck. She'd moved his goddamn truck! Her fingerprints, all over it. How would she explain that?

Maybe he *had* woken up. Hungover, depressed. Maybe he did it to himself. But two *days* later? No. Someone had started the fire, and it wasn't Kemp. Besides, he thought too highly of himself to ever do anything like that.

"He was seen up on the roof sometime before the blaze," Lumen said. "Only he wasn't alone. The man who saw him said he was with someone. A woman."

"Ali?" Sarah wondered.

"No. That's the strange thing. The woman doesn't fit the description of Ali Washington."

"Oh?" Sarah said, thoughts racing. What had happened? But then something new crept in. Adam tiptoeing out to care for Maddie on Thursday night. He had turned off the baby monitor. What had he told her, the night before the fire? *I want you to know that I'm going to take care of it. I'm going to take care of everything.*

He had done something. He had done *this* for her. Her tongue was loosening up. Her mind was clearing. *Adam* had saved her. Sent it all up in the sky. Now it was her turn. Back and forth. A baton. She felt dizzy with love. They would win. She would make sure they would win. So, she had to do this right. She had to do this exactly right.

"He must have been mixed up," Sarah said. "He thinks he saw me up on the roof? Can you imagine? Late at night? When I have school to teach? I have a *baby* at home. Can you imagine? What would *I* be doing up there? On a *roof*?"

"Well," Detective Lumen said thoughtfully. "Your principal, Evie Kemp, says you *did* seem out of sorts that morning. She mentioned you looked tired, and she said you were dressed unusually, in purple and pink. She said that she noticed you came to school without makeup and that you had a bruise, right there." Lumen leaned out a little, pointing to Sarah's cheek.

Sarah laughed. "Not everyone can afford to dress like Evie Kemp. Not everyone has a millionaire husband, and not everyone has the time to put on perfect makeup."

"And the bruise?" Prichard wondered. "What's the story there?"

Sarah looked at him, a little hurt. He'd dropped his incompetence act, and she realized how much it had comforted her. Just another failing-upward man, her underqualified escape hatch. But also, there was peanut butter on the corner of his lip, evidence of a hurried breakfast. Used to be that parents with children with peanut allergies were the best parents around. Look! So attentive. Now, it was reversed. If your kid was allergic to George Washington Carver's favorite nut, it was because you hadn't exposed them early enough. You had failed. The whole script flipped, and flipped again. It always would.

"I . . ." What did they say was a good lie? Something with truth mixed in? "I do it to myself. I poke my cheek." She was whispering. This was the first time she'd told this to anyone. Tears sprang to her eyes, rolled fat-backed down her cheeks. "Sometimes, I don't know why, but since my baby, I'll catch myself poking my finger into my cheek. I don't know. I know it's not healthy. They call it postpartum anxiety, or depression."

"Oh?" Prichard said.

"I'm sorry," Lumen said.

"Evie Kemp mentioned your name," Prichard said. "She mentioned you right away when she heard about the description of the woman on the roof. She seems to be under the impression that you and her son had a situation going on. Why would she think that?"

"I don't know," Sarah said. "I don't know anything about why Evie Kemp does *anything*. She sends me pictures of herself, really inappropriate pictures, and she's always buying me gifts. I don't know. She's obsessed with me, I think."

"Obsessed?" Lumen looked down at her pad.

"Listen," Sarah said, opening up her phone, searching through her thread for the photos Evie had sent. "I don't know what Sam saw, but it wasn't me."

"You know his name?"

"Who's name?"

"Sam?" Detective Lumen said. "You said the name of the gentleman who claims to have seen Crispin on the roof is Sam."

"The houseless man." Great, thick drops of sweat rolled down her side. She would smell terrible. Perhaps already did. What was the evolutionary intent of such a thing? There had to be one. The body, as she was taught to understand it, was simply a manifestation of responses to stresses. Were Prichard's nostrils flaring? What good did smelling like a hamburger do for her now?

"Did we mention he was homeless?" Lumen said.

"You did, I think."

"I don't know if we did," Prichard said.

"Well, I just assumed," Sarah said. "He's well-known in the neighborhood. He's constantly out there. Some people call him Tin Can Sam. He's always shouting about peanut butter cunts. Was it not him? I just assumed." Careful. Careful now. "You know, Sam gets mixed up a lot."

"OK . . ." Lumen said.

God, Sarah needed towels. Dab under each arm. She found the photos. She thrust her phone forward. Prichard took it and showed it to Lumen.

"OK," Prichard said. "Can you send these to us?"

"Sure," Sarah said, taking her phone back. "Of course."

"But he says he saw someone of your description with Kemp on the roof. And Evie Kemp says the morning after someone of your description was on the roof, late at night, that you showed up to work looking worse for wear. Like you hadn't slept much. Do you understand what I'm wondering here?"

"Oh—" Sarah looked into her hands. Sell this. Her burden. "Well, I *did* see Crispin recently. But it was *not* on a roof, and certainly it *wasn't* at night." She chuckled to herself. Dry, humorless. "Like I said, I'm a teacher. And a new mom. I have to get sleep or the kids eat me alive."

"Right, but why were you in so early?" Lumen took out a notebook and hunted with her finger. "Evie Kemp says that ever since you've had the baby, you arrive around eight in the morning. She says on *that* day, your badge has you scanning in at 6:07."

Fucking Evie Kemp.

"I had some things to take care of. Listen, I've been cutting it really close this year. I just needed a morning when I could get in early, before anyone else, and take care of things. I'm just so tired. I'm so tired of just barely holding it together, so I thought, if I could just take care of a few things, get some stuff off my plate, I could get it all back together."

Lumen wasn't convinced, and God, she was so beautiful. She was almost painful to look at. And Kemp was dead. Dead. Dead. Maybe by her mouth, maybe by Adam's hand.

"So when did Sam see you with Crispin?" Detective Lumen asked. "If it wasn't that night, then when was this?

"Yes," Sarah said, squinching her face up to show Lumen she was thinking. "It was a few days ago. Sometime last week? Wednesday or Thursday?"

"Can you tell me more about that?"

"Yes, well. Sometimes Crispin and I talked when we saw each other. Just whatever stuff. He'd ask me about Ali, I'd ask him about his mom. Advice, you know? She's very . . . difficult. So I ran into him that day, and we were talking about Ali, because they had just broken up."

"Do you have his phone number?" Lumen said. "Would you call each other? Text?"

A simple question, and Sarah knew she had to answer quickly. They could get her phone records. Couldn't they get her phone records? But only if they suspected that they needed to get her phone records. A request for a warrant and then . . . It wasn't even Kemp's phone, but those random numbers. These thoughts—the mind was a wonder—were all firing simultaneously as she answered without hesitation, instinct taking the wheel.

"No, never anything like that."

"OK, so on that day . . ." Lumen prompted.

"So, yes, that day we were talking about Ali. He was pretty upset and carrying out some of his things. He was crying, but his hands were full, I remember that, and he was crying, but, like, he couldn't wipe his eyes because his hands were full. I felt, well, *sorry* for him."

Sarah stopped, as if lost in memory. But she was wondering if she was being too detailed. Did people get into trouble for lying because they were too vague or because they were too detailed? She decided it was somewhere in the middle. Besides, so much of this *was* real. She *had* talked to Kemp as he packed up, he *had* been crying. Only it wasn't for Ali. It was for her.

"I can't *really* remember too clearly," she said. "Maddie's been going through a sleep regression."

"Did he seem suicidal?" Lumen said.

"I mean, I don't know," Sarah said. "He seemed really sad, but I didn't think he would do anything like that. Otherwise . . ." Real emotion entered Sarah. Kemp had been a lot of things, but he had been great in some ways too, hadn't he? Passionate, smart, and God, was he handsome. She hadn't wanted him to *die*. She used that. Channeled it. Real in the service of unreal. "If I'd known that something like this was going to happen. If I'd known that he was so broken up about it that he might . . . of course I would have tried to get him help."

"And Sam saw you, when this interchange was happening?"

"Yes, he came by—but he's always coming by."

"But this was earlier in the week, correct?"

"Sometime, sure," Sarah said. "I can't remember which day exactly."

"What day do you put out your recycling?" Detective Lumen asked.

"Wednesday," Sarah said. "What does that—"

"Was it Wednesday? When you saw Sam, was it Wednesday?"

Sarah flew blind: "I don't know. Like I said, maybe, but maybe not. It might have been another day. He's always going down our street. Different neighborhoods have different days, and he's always going down our streets. I think even just across César Chávez they have a different pickup day."

"You seem to know a lot about recycling."

The bell rang, and students filled the halls. She had one more free period coming up. She would go to the pumping room. She felt her breasts heavy and eager with the upcoming work. "I need to pump. Can we pick this up another time?"

"Mrs. Cooper?"

"Yes?"

"You said that when you saw him last he was distraught but had an armful of things he was moving out."

"That's right."

"Sam, the homeless man, you said he saw you then. But what exactly did he see? It was his impression that . . . Well, what exactly happened the last time you saw him?"

"Well, I told Crispin it would be alright. I told him breakups were inevitable, we've all been through them. I told him he would find someone else. He was so young. Then I opened the door to his truck for him, so he could put the boxes in."

Lumen stepped in, alert, as if she'd just been hit with the scent of blood.

"So he took out his keys, and—"

"No," Sarah said. "His hands were full. He has one of those doors with the combos on the door handle? So he just told me the code and I opened it up. Then I helped him load his things." Her fingerprints could be all over that car. She was *helping* him in his time of need. "After that, I hugged him. He seemed like he needed it. And then he left."

"Oh," Detective Lumen said. "Do you happen to remember that code?"

"No," Sarah said. "Of course not. I was just trying to help him. I was just trying to do the right thing."

35

Adam

THE NIGHT THAT Ali and her roommates left for their
bachelorette party, Adam waited for Maddie's crying
over the monitor to draw him from bed. He needed this to
be like any other night.

Only Maddie's crying didn't come. Some luck. This
might be the night when Maddie finally returned to sleeping through. Adam was lying there, rigid, fear creeping
up his throat. A few more days and Kemp's disappearance
would be obvious. How wasn't it already? Wasn't his work
curious? His mother? Was that why she had come by with
the smoothie? The crows. Wouldn't local authorities be
alerted to the crows? But again, Kemp was in Seattle. He
was supposed to be in Seattle. So maybe . . . but Adam
knew the vermin would increase. That family of squirrels
he'd seen. Come, children, feast! Evie Kemp had noticed
the birds. She had taken a picture.

Who else might begin to notice? It took a lot these
days for anyone to notice anything outside their little

box of light. God, how many hours had he spent watching Ali undress in the window? Anticipating it? Following
lookalikes down rabbit holes? But it would come to the
point where the crows were undeniable. Or the smell. The
body would be found, and his wife would be caught up in
it. Whatever she had done. It would catch them all up in it.
They hadn't even paid off their remodel. They might *never*
pay off their remodel.

Unless . . .

Still, no noise from below. Maddie was sound asleep,
so there was no reason for him to get up. And he needed
a reason. He needed to make it so Sarah would never have
to lie.

And into this tension, Adam felt Sarah's hand slide
across the expanse. Funny, he hadn't even tried. For the
first time in months sex, or the bitter lack of it, had not
crossed his mind. But she put her palm on his chest. She
shifted closer, head on his shoulder.

"Sarah," he said, before he could stop himself. "I just
want you to know."

"What," she said, in this little thimbleful voice. "We don't
have to go into it, Adam. Let's just try not going into it."

"I want you to know that I'm going to take care of it,"
he said. "I'm going to take care of everything."

She laughed, or she coughed, or she clucked somewhere in the back of her throat.

"Really?" she finally said, her hand traveling down. He
lay still, as if any movement might lift the spell. She had
cheated on him. She had been with Kemp—this thought
came unbidden—but he was relieved, and also annoyed,
that it did nothing to subvert his erection.

"Are you going to take care of it for me?"

His mind cast about. She had said that what hurt the most when she saw him staring at Ali through the window was the obvious *emotional* connection between them. That was worse than any physical cheating he might have done. Adam was closed off to her, but had opened up and received from this almost-stranger phantom in the glass. For Adam, it was the opposite. Typical, he guessed, of a male. Penis and skin. It was the fact that *her* body was being touched, tasted, had by someone else. Her feeling, moving, doing with another. So they had both hurt each other in the worst possible way.

But, he also realized they had, or were about to, risk everything *for* each other.

"I'm going to take care of it all," he said.

This was their way back.

She bit his ear; she pulled at his sweats. He helped her, wiggling them down, and she climbed on top. She was already there. Salty, the skin beneath her breast. He buried his nose in her armpit. That scent. An odor he knew. A decade together. He knew. He was furious with action. Before Maddie, they had always been sweet, echoing back and forth meaningless endearments. And he'd loved her, but this was more. They would do anything for each other. Those weren't just words any longer. He reached up, grabbed her breasts, swollen and leaking from the nipples.

"I'm sorry," she said.

"It's OK," he told her, and he put his mouth over one, and then the other. So sweet and strange what came from her. "This is what I want."

Afterward, they lay for a minute, maybe less, Adam's mind a complete roar of white blankness. It was embarrassing, the time just after, thinking back on all that you had allowed yourself to do and say. He was sticky and wet. He tasted milk. *Her* milk. He lapped it up like a deviant. He had been eager to the point of cartoonishness. *I want your pussy. I want to split you in half.* Adam knew better than most the difference between outside and in. You kept the ugly parts to yourself. And yet, what was sex for. *It's for you*, Sarah said to him. *It's your fucking pussy.* Sex was for removing the barrier. What was outside was in. And what was inside was out. He wasn't embarrassed any longer. If you weren't getting there, he realized, you were having sex wrong. Check once, check again, and then a third time, because it was worth it. He felt happy.

Then Maddie took up her wail after all, laying claim, finally, to the night. Once more, at least. One last time. They were all in it together.

"I'll go," Sarah said, half asleep.

"No," he told her. "You let me sleep in this weekend and we'll call it even."

"Of course," Sarah said, a boat already gone to sea. "Of course we'll be even."

He went downstairs and turned off the monitor. It would be silent in their room. Then, Adam closed the door on his daughter and let her cry.

He went to work.

He took cotton balls and Vaseline from the medicine cabinet. He massaged the oil into the cotton until they were sodden, wet, and cold in his fingers. Then he sawed off the top of a milk carton with their bread knife. It was an old backpacking trick he'd learned on one of those climbing trips he used to take. Mr. June. Dirt and tangled hair. Weak weed and cheap vodka. Sunrises and moments of tingling vividness. He would start those up again. With better supplies. He'd been SAHD in all the wrong ways. From here on out, he would be the father that took his daughter out on weekday camping trips. She would come up summer tan and forest-wild. Who cared if you made money. Deathbeds and all. Money wasn't what people were talking about there. Everyone said that. And everyone couldn't be wrong.

He looked at his little creation. You could start a fire in a rainstorm with these. In fact, he *had* started fires in rainstorms with these. But Adam needed it delayed. Whoosh right up and he'd be caught there, on the roof, with the dead body and matches. So he went to the rhododendron bush in the backyard. An animal—a rat?—scurried away in the dark. Adam picked leaves, ten, fifteen to be sure, dark green and full of water, and he stuffed them into the bottom of the carton. Then he put the cotton balls on top.

When they had moved into their house, the previous owner had left some of her old junk behind. Their realtor told them that he could contact the seller and insist she clear it all, but Adam and Sarah declined. They were so happy just to have the keys that they couldn't bear the thought of ceding it back to someone even for a day. In the garage were a pitchfork, gardening gloves, a rusted tin can filled with nails and screws, and two jugs of gasoline.

He took one of these, the biggest, and on that black night he walked down their street, far enough from Tina's house that he wouldn't trigger the floodlight, crossed, and crept back to Ali's house in the dark. Nobody was awake; nobody was around. The girls were all gone. Even the crows seemed to be sleeping. Adam studied every window he could see to be sure nobody was up and watching as he had once been. Then he climbed the trellis, up the laurel, at the side of her house. Slow and quiet, the jug of gas a heavy chore. But he could do this. He was a good climber. His old skills came back to him. He pressed his body close to the side of the house. He made sure to use his legs. When he gained the roof, a huge form, almost as big as a man, King Crow, rose from Kemp's body and into the sky with blundering wing strokes. He watched it go, waiting ten seconds, fifteen to be sure. Then he went to the body, trying not to look too closely at the torn, eaten flesh. Here was a person, a son. He had things, wanted things, did things. Two lives, three. The online self, the work self, the man who'd stolen his wife and neighbor both.

Adam tore up shingles around the body and ripped through the tar paper to expose the plywood sheathing. Next, he unscrewed the cap on the gasoline slightly and then set the jug on its side, upward on the pitch from Kemp. The clear, pungent liquid seeped forth, running down the roof tiles, reaching out toward the body. He put the milk carton on Kemp's shoulder. The house would burn down. Nobody would be hurt since all the girls were gone, and their pasts would go up in smoke. He felt a pang of regret when he thought about the future and the trauma something like this might engender within them. A whole house. Would they forever be checking the stove like he was? Would they buy fire extinguishers for their new homes and put them in every room? Would they have nightmares in their marital beds? Was he giving Ali something she would carry around for the rest of her life? No, Adam decided. Ali was stronger than that.

He lit the cotton balls. They bloomed merrily with warm light. The leaves beneath them smoked, wet and resistant. He stepped back and judged his work. There was an itch in his brain, a perverse twist of his anxiety, usually tuned to catching the dangerous, nullifying it, and soothing it. He had the thought that he should put the fire out and then light it again, just to be sure. Or, perhaps he should make another cotton-ball starter entirely. Could you ever be sure? Check once, and again, and again. Enough. He had had enough. This would catch, or it wouldn't. They would be free, or they wouldn't. They were both in it, either way. Still, he felt that nervous jump within him to overhandle circumstances. And still, it didn't matter. *Sit over there*, he told those thoughts. *Sit over there and let me work.*

He fished in Kemp's jacket, took out his phone. Kemp's cold, bluish hand gave up the thumbprint that opened the device. Almost out of battery now. Adam swished over to Safari. He was proud to have picked out gloves that could work on an iPhone screen. No fingerprints here. He tapped in Ali's blog address. On her most recent post, the one that seemed to say she was leaving, he commented in Kemp's name and pressed publish. Then, he wiped the phone down with a Clorox wipe that had been kissing his thigh damp through his pocket and, by far the hardest thing he had to do that whole night, tucked the phone back into Kemp's tight jeans. He tried to not look at his face, but saw it now. Its gray smile was ripped wide, eyes gone. It would stay with him, forever, and he considered it right, to pay this price.

Adam stood up, watched the small glow, turned in a slow circle, scanning the street. He thought, for a brief, startled moment, that he saw movement in his bedroom window across the street. But no. It was nothing. Life mimicking in the shadows on the glass.

Adam showered, sitting in the tub, soaping and rinsing again and again. He had to get everything off him. Every smell, every fiber. His mind was beginning to kick into its old saw: *what could go wrong, something will go wrong, what could go wrong, something will* . . . The room crowded with steam. His stomach was an abyss. His skin was wrinkling and wilting. Pruned too close to the quick. Maybe he'd never get up again. He let out short, stippled breaths.

Then he realized something. Maddie wasn't crying. He'd come in from Ali's house and everything was quiet. Adam turned off the shower. He put his clothes in the washer, sanitary cycle, and he crept into his daughter's room. She was fast asleep. Peaceful, red-faced, an angel. She had cried herself out. She would sleep through this night. From here on out, she would sleep through every night. She was a miracle. Plump, smooth skin. A gauzy brush of soft hair. Full of hormones with superhero names like Relaxin. She was everything.

For a while, back in the wobbly nighttime light of their bedroom, Adam sat near the window and watched Ali's house. Any moment, he knew, he hoped, the house would dance up, a grounded star, heat and light.

Sarah stirred. "Come to bed."

Adam should have stayed up and worried the rest of the blue morning through. *It might not light, it might not go, your fingerprints, it might not light, it might not go, your fingerprints* . . . His obsessive brain, a minority shout, insisted, demanded. But there were still hours left to sleep and someone to share those with. He climbed into bed and let Sarah enfold him in her arms.

CHAPTER

36

Ali

THAT THURSDAY NIGHT, Ali waited until the party died down. Until the women were all asleep, every last one. Good night, Good night, sweet princesses. Until each dick necklace was cast aside, and every vodka bottle cashed. Then she got into her car and drove away from the audacious rental house on the river and away from those brides-to-be, the stupid games and the bright-pink sashes. Someone's brought weed gummies! No *way*. Then there were the glow and smear of slushy margaritas so sweet her gums ached, wine teeth, finger foods, and then—what the fuck, if nobody else will do it, she would—pizza! Greasy, lay-back pizza. It wasn't good, but that wasn't the point. There were stories from the women already married and hopes from those yet to be. But mostly, they recalled memories from their wild past. Can you believe it? Can you even imagine how stupid we were!

She couldn't stand it, so she left.

It was predawn, blue-black, when she arrived back on Salmon Street. Right away, she saw the smoke and the small gnome of flame tap-dancing on the roof. Ali had never loved the house. It leaned to the side so much that if you put a tennis ball under her window, you would have to race it to the door. Its walls were too skinny. It was too hot in the summer and too cold in the winter. The electricity was shoddy. Once, she had opened the breaker box, trying to figure out the root of a power failure to the outlets in the kitchen, and closed it right back up when she saw what appeared to be rows of glass knobs like this was some kind of Jules Verne spacecraft. If you cranked the heat, all you got was an anemic ghost going through the motions, teasing you. Tina and her parties. Charlie and her hippy magic. Mrs. Jenkins always reminding her that once upon a time the people who lived there had raspberries, the most delicious raspberries—they really took care of it. Adam and Kemp. That window. That cursed window.

Her young twenties. The time of her life. Such a fun age. She hated it.

Ali knew there would be real loss: photos gone that meant something, a collection of diaries salted beneath her bed, the materials, with the outrageous cost of inks and lights and screens, her sketches and concepts, her prints. Gone, gone, gone. A shared recognition that, whatever else happened tonight, *this* moment was going to capstone everything. We hate bad things. We tack our boats on dangerous trajectories to break away from them, and yet, when all is said and done, as long as they aren't truly horrific, they are all we talk about.

If she let it go, it would be a kind of trauma. A blackened wreckage. But, Ali knew that house, and the fact that it had just managed to adequately roof her was the last thing bonding her to this place. To these people. To this act. She could stop it. She could call it in right now, and the firemen wouldn't have any problem putting it out.

Instead, she put her car in gear. Goodbye, goodbye to all of that. She would make an early, unplanned visit home to California for Thanksgiving. She would never leave again. She got lost and found herself across the Hawthorne Bridge, turning past the courthouse building under construction with the huddled masses out front, the most ill-served of all. Finally, she found I-5. Let's go California hunting.

Later, the detectives will get ahold of her. Later, they will ask about Kemp. Later, she will learn that the theory is that Kemp, in a fit of depression or heartbreak, had burned himself alive. Nobody could get ahold of him, and his work had finally stopped being pushed to the servers. Also, he'd left a comment on her blog. Everyone seemed to think this was a big deal.

"He wasn't exactly . . ." Ali will say, though she'll suspect it doesn't matter. She didn't even know that he knew about her blog. He had never been all that interested in her, anyway. "Him and me, it was just for fun, you know? We were never really serious." She will feel bad for clarifying his lack of importance, this man who had just died. Or, will she? He will be gone, and she will be in shock.

On the Zoom screen, Detective Lumen will tilt her head, look at her like, *Yeah, I get it,* but Prichard beside her will seem genuinely confused.

"He had a key to your house," Prichard will say.

"He wasn't supposed to. It was just from this time he was watering my plants. He was supposed to give it back. You think he was really *that* upset about me?"

"It's hard to know," Detective Lumen will tell her. "What something means to one person and what that same thing means to another can be worlds apart. Was there any indication that he was in a different state of mind?"

So Ali will tell them about the encounter by the bus stop, the insistent texts, and his car lurking on her street. She will give them Candice's number. Her sisters', too. Just ask them. She had told them what was going on. And, after a little prodding, she will even tell them about the package of drugs that had shown up at her work. The Logicstyx sticker. She expects that they might push back on her; that maybe they won't believe it. Instead, they both will nod as if this were something they'd been waiting for her to say.

"Thank you," Detective Prichard will say. "You're really helping us paint a clearer picture."

"Enjoy your visit in LA," Lumen will tell her.

Then she will close the screen and remember Kemp from the first time she saw him. Dancing at The Turtle on 2000s hip-hop night. It was a sweaty hole under Lonely Heart's Pizza with a low ceiling and pillars throughout, so you were constantly losing people in corners. Ja Rule was demanding J-Lo spell out his motherfucking name when she went up for air. This was when he chose to appear, glasses and a grin, wanting to know if she had a cigarette and "the numerical digits for your cellular device."

"Yeah, right," she told him. But it was an act. She wasn't noticed in this place. She wasn't special. It was nice to be picked out. "Yeah, right."

She hit the gas. *Follow me south*, the road sang beneath her tires. All the way home. Ali was moving back home. To LA. Like right now. She had nothing to pack. She stopped at Oak Grove Rest Area outside Eugene and emailed her notice and texted Candice goodbye. She got ahold of Mel Sweetney, who seemed sad about it but assured her that she could still work on the posters. In fact, Mel had contacts in LA. She would set Ali up. And so, all Ali had to do was drive her shitty Saturn with the droopy bumper and crank windows. And what was a car except a reason to go? It seemed to her they had all been using this extraordinary tool for the wrong thing, shuttling from one monotony to the next. A car was for grand movement. Big getaways. She would go to LA, where there was a bigger struggle to get the small things but also more sunshine and no more of this rain. You figured when it rained this much, at least you didn't have to worry about your house burning down. But there you had it. Your house could burn down.

She could have stopped that fire, but she didn't. It wasn't hers to put out. If she drove straight through, she'd be at her parents' house tonight. And that was what she needed. People, real people, with nothing between them at all.

The insurance will pay her a lump sum in the end for all her burned belongings. At the time, Roommate One or Roommate Two insisted it was a good plan. She had thought of it as a waste of money, and she had been wrong. It gives her the funds she needs to start fresh in Los Angeles. More than enough. She will rent an apartment with a bathtub to take nighttime soaks with the windows open. Her blinds, ancient silk, will be thin as ghost skin, fluttering in a jasmine breeze. She will take Mel's loose list of tangential contacts and mold it into self-sustainability. She'll do commissions, murals, the wall on the side of a grocery store off La Brea Avenue, just up from Pink's Hot Dogs. It will be a first step. Walking to running until her art is selling for bigger and bigger amounts on SuperRare. co.NFT. Ethereum something.

And her knee will ache a little less each day. The warmer weather will be good for it. Yes, something in there had been torn or sprained or misaligned that rainy day when Kemp tried to hang on to her at the bus stop. A reminder. A warning. But the discomfort will shrink, less and less shrill, all the time.

And after her baths, she will lie in bed as the heat radiates off of her. Then she will pull out her phone and tweet or gram. She will have cachet by then. She will have numbers. Remember? Remember how, once upon a time, she'd been impressed by that little blue check next to Kemp's profile? Now she has it too.

can't sleep, she might write. jasmine too beautiful

She'll lay the phone beside her and close her eyes. When she wakes up, her phone will be filled with responses. Reply guys and next-ups. She will have sway. She will be cool. Anytime she writes anything, people will post their best responses below. All auditioning for her. All hungry for that red heart love she might tap out to them through her tiny window.

37

Sarah

E VIE FOUND HER in the nursing room, that small, dim
space where even the posters were giving up.

"Oh," Sarah said when the woman entered. This time,
she was already buttoned back up, her machine packed
neatly away, her milk take for that day—a bumper crop,
over five ounces!—securely lidded and ready to go. She
watched Evie's face as she realized that Sarah was finally
wearing the sweater she'd given her from R13. Did it send
a message? Sarah could see by the tightening of Evie's lips
that it did. But the right one? "Principal Kemp."

Sarah imagined Evie would be like she always was.
Controlled. Smart. Probing for weakness. Instead, she
blurted out right away, shaky and deranged, "How long
were you and my son seeing each other."

Sarah took in a small breath of surprise. "I don't know
what you're talking about!"

She did a good job of acting shocked. Mr. Monroe, her
high school drama teacher, would have been proud. That

flicker of her eyelids, even the intake of breath, were a nice touch. But Evie didn't buy it.

"You were fucking Crispin," Evie said.

"I don't know what you're talking about," Sarah said again, but this time in a rote, low monotone.

Evie took another step and her foot was on the strap of Sarah's bag. Sarah tugged at it, once, then sat back and looked up, a long way to go. Evie was at least a foot taller than her. She could crush her. Sarah could see what this woman was built with, clenched fists aside: turns of phrase, of fortune, of luck. She intimidated and she charmed. She gathered emotional friction and charged her batteries. All of that rage traveled down into her hand. It seemed red and pulsing with energy begging to be used. Sarah looked at her. She *welcomed* this. She *needed* this to happen. She presented her face to this woman. This would be the last time a Kemp would hurt her.

"I don't know what you're talking—"

And Evie did it. She lashed out, the strength summoned from a primordial pool accessible to those in need only once or twice in their lives. She struck Sarah's face, caught some of the flyaway hairs along her neck. Sarah felt the splash of pain, the pricks of hair yanked free of their follicles. They all said Evie was pretty, including the other teachers. Adam even noticed it. She's incredible, this principal. She's stylish and smart and she *cares*. Sarah didn't think so. In fact, Evie *wasn't* all that pretty. She was makeup and clothes and causes. She was an effect. She was money. She was a filter on a social media app. Sarah let her face slack to the side from the tingle and pressure. And then, slowly, she came back to balance. Should she smile? No, too much. No smiling. Evie had struck the exact place on Sarah's cheek she had abused these last few months with her finger. The skin took its role beautifully. Black and blue all over. Already she could feel Evie's slap ripening on her pale skin. It would only worsen. The perfect match for one hand.

"Shhhh," Sarah said.

Evie gasped. She seemed to be having trouble breathing.

"Shhhh," Sarah kept on. The shadows in that place were sharp and delineating, impressions of movement as the light swung back and forth. She transformed from monster to victim to woman as if Sarah might become anything she wanted to.

"You better keep it down," Sarah said. "You wouldn't want people to hear."

"You were fucking my son," Evie said again, although it was quieter now. She'd come free of whatever strength she'd managed to access, a taproot severed from the earth. "And he was a little much, and so you . . . you . . . you . . . you pushed him to do it, you made him do it."

"I wonder, what do you think the detectives will make of you? Those texts you sent me, they already have them. But what do you think they'll think about this? I should check the cameras in my house and show them what I find. What might I find, Evie? We have them there to keep an eye on Maddie. What else might they have picked up?"

"You don't . . . I have . . ."

There were no cameras, but Evie didn't know this. Evie was done knowing anything.

"I love this sweater, by the way," Sarah said. "So soft."

"You don't know what you're talking about," Evie said.

Sarah stood up and brushed past her, yanking free her bag so roughly Evie tripped into the chair. Evie hit her elbow on the back of the seat and yelped in pain.

"I want you to know that I'm not the reason Crispin died," Sarah said.

"But, Sarah, he wouldn't do that."

"You know Crispin," Sarah said. "You know he would do whatever he thought it took. And he just went too far this time. That's all it was. He just went too far. He was so sad about Ali. You've seen the comment he left on her blog, haven't you?"

"He was so smart and determined," Evie said.

"I'll be out through December." Sarah took out her phone, reversed the camera, and assessed her cheek. It was bruising quickly. She took a photo, and there was a brief flash of light. "It will give us both time to heal."

"But . . ." Evie said. And her voice was so weak that Sarah knew she wouldn't do a thing. Evie Kemp was nothing if not smart. She saw the board. She played her position. She would inherit Crispin's Logicstyx windfall and the tragic gravity of her loss. She would have everything.

"Oh, and thank you for the smoothie," Sarah said. "But next time, it's a little inconsiderate to run down someone's vibrator like that. It's almost like you weren't thinking of anyone but yourself."

38

Adam

THEY HEADED TO the coast. The detectives had asked their questions. They said to stay available, stay local. And Adam and Sarah would. They decided, what, an hour and a half away? Two at the most. The beach wasn't too far. Thanksgiving on the sand. They were still "local." They weren't "making a getaway." Ali had driven all the way to California for God's sake.

Adam packed Maddie up, Sarah made lunch, and they drove out of Portland, onto Highway 6, in the middle of the day. Smooth, gray asphalt under gray gauzy skies. Blank, blank, blank. He had earbuds in, and so did Sarah. It was their custom while driving. Listen to something while Maddie slept. If they talked, it would only risk waking their daughter. Only Adam hadn't tapped his bud to turn anything on yet. The podcast or playlist or audiobook sat patiently, waiting for if and when it was needed. Back of head, back of mind. Banks, the turnoff for Vernonia, wet woods and small, huddled, end-of-the-world houses.

MAGA banners and signs saying TRESPASSERS WILL
BE SHOT.

The highway climbed and climbed, a tension building, until it broke at the pass, 3,631 feet above the sea.
Then it sluiced down and ran through Tillamook Forest,
thick with trees and fuzzy with moss. The highway met up
like a wandering tributary with the Wilson River. The two
pathways, one ancient, one temporary, took the generous
bends in tandem, never to touch, but dancing, knowing
the choreography perfectly.

Every turnout and trailhead from there on was clotted
with cars. Men and women in hip waders threaded line
into their poles. The salmon running up would need luck,
skill, and belief to make it through all those hooks. They
had a slim chance of getting home.

But *nobody* had much more than slim chances. It was
all any of us could count on. And some, in the end, do
make it. It's rarely the righteous, the deserving.

Adam reached out and held Sarah's hand. She looked
at him and smiled, grotesque with the blackening bruise on
her face. It was better than it looked, Sarah insisted. They'd
taken photos, cataloged obsessively. People would assume
it was Adam who had hit her. Poor lady, can't defend herself. To think of Sarah as defenseless was laughable. Maddie
was fascinated by the wound, touching it solemnly whenever Sarah nursed her. She would heal soon. She'd never
looked more fierce. She was beautiful, in her way. He asked
her what happened. This whole business was shady. A fire
across the street. A suicide. A bruise on her face.

I was looking up, Sarah had told him. *I was looking up
when I wasn't supposed to be, when I should have been looking where I was going.*

It didn't explain the time off or the change in her demeanor, but he let her have it. Because sometimes you let your partner have it. Benefit of the doubt. Ugly turns. Desperate acts. Both of them held secrets; both of them were more honest with each other than they'd ever been. What he was finding out, more and more every day, was that marriage wasn't the beautiful union of two unfinished souls finishing each other. It was a pact. A deal. I'll show you all of mine because I've seen all of yours.

And Maddie would forget all of it. Their child would grow up and only see two devoted people graying into old age, a love to be emulated.

A huge pickup pulled out from a gravel offshoot behind them, spraying black rock. It roared to gain highway speed and pressed up against Adam's bumper, a few feet off, making it clear that he wasn't going fast enough. Or maybe he'd read the stickers on Adam's back window and didn't appreciate the Green New Deal or Black Lives Matter. Maddie babbled awake in the back seat, one of her sounds that almost came off as a word, like apple, bug, or dog. Or the big ones: mama, dada. Soon she would be talking. Soon she would take up her job of describing the world. But for now, she was supposed to be sleeping.

"It's OK," Adam told her, finding her chubby face in the rearview. "This is just an asshole."

The truck's headlights were custom-made. A green, vertical line ran down the center of each white eye. Adam imagined this man in a camo hat, finding these while standing in line at an auto parts store, enraptured.

They were so cool! So beautiful! They would make the girl he liked want him back!

A small vanity, a bead in a string of small vanities, lusted over until obtained and then discarded into a pile of evidence proving that none of it mattered all that much after all.

Unless you were careful.

Unless you were brave.

Unless . . . unless . . . unless . . .

Adam had texted Ali that morning. One more time before deleting her number.

I hope you make it safe. wherever you're going.

Because she had vanished for real this time. Her roommates had come by and asked if he had known about her plans. *No, no, no. Of course not. We weren't that close, really.*

Her house was black, charred dust. The lot, rumor had it, already had an interested buyer. A developer was planning on crowding in three skinny homes. New construction. An upgrade for the street. All the property values increasing, forever increasing. They would be richer and richer, and they wouldn't have to do a thing.

He didn't know if they would ever talk about what happened through those windows, what everyone was doing, but it didn't matter. The things we are obsessed with, the flickers in the shadows, the plays in the light, the dramas we lust for, and the people we wish we were. The things we dream, the little while-away moments of fantasy and hope and despair. The things we can look back on and chuckle about. Oh, what silly people we were. There is a ticking clock in each of us counting down to when we finally open our eyes. And some never do.

But Adam had.

The yellow line broke into dashes, and the truck behind them roared as if these were a trail of crumbs to gobble. It slashed into the oncoming lane, unwound every horse within, and glanced past them. Adam saw, through the tinted window, a mesh cap and a bored, destructive face. But, just as this man was clearing their front tire, Adam accelerated, not letting him in, unraveling every bit of his engine too. He pinned the truck in the oncoming lane as a van from the other direction approached, honking furiously. The truck swerved, caught there, and Adam looked at him, dancing cheek to cheek, clammy skin and clenched jaw, hands jerky on the wheel. The truck wobbled, skidded, and seemed about to tip over completely. The stupid man had jacked it up beyond reason, and the vehicle sat upon its suspension like the jiggling gelatin flourish on a dessert. All this stupid boy had to do was slow down, but Adam knew the spell he was under, the one they were all under, and this man would not back down. And so, he had given himself to Adam. His hands ached with pleasure. A trill within his scrotal septum, ringing up into a network of glands he didn't know he had. A beat, two. That was all. That was more than enough to teach this man beside him the song. Then he tapped his brakes and the truck regained itself, jabbed over in front of Adam just in time, the howling of the van searing the day, whooshing past. After a wallowing moment of shock, the truck lit off, running hard, Adam was sure, to whatever sodden corner of fantasy he carved out for himself.

"I appreciate you driving," Sarah said, smiling at him, watching him the whole time, always now.

"And I appreciate you," he told her.

She laughed. "You're supposed to tell me for what. That's what the therapist said. To make it specific."

"For everything," he said. They had just had their first session online. They were working on their communication. "For everything you're willing to do to make this family work."

She laughed again. It was the most beautiful thing in the world. "You too," she said. There had never been more love in her voice. "You too."

Oh, we're all the same. We're all the same until we decide to be different. Sarah patted his knee, hand sliding up to his crotch, just briefly, a promise to fulfill later, and then turned in her seat to sing Maddie to sleep with a lullaby.

"You are my sunshine, my only sunshine . . ."

He checked the rearview mirror and saw his baby. Then he checked again. And a third time. He closed his eyes and imagined Ali's house on fire. It bloomed with heat and dancing light. Then he opened his eyes again and saw only the open road. He reached up and tapped the earbud and let everything in.

ACKNOWLEDGMENTS

THANKS TO:

Kesey. You are a thoughtful, story-loving, creative powerhouse of a son. You're only eight and already too much for me to handle on the basketball court. I love you and I am very proud of you.

Clay. You are a hilarious, bright, wake-everyone-up-before-the-sun-rises, turbo-charged engine of a six-year-old son. You once told me a joke that, to this day, is still the funniest thing I've ever heard. I love you and I am very proud of you.

Rachael Dillon Fried for getting the band back together. What a journey!

Kristin Brown for generous eyes, genius suggestions, and warm encouragement.

Kashann Kilson for listening to me whine when this was out on submission and for the clutch, last-second, smart-as-hell read.

My siblings, Abi, Ackley, and Sydney—I lucked out getting to come up with you all.

My parents, two wonderful examples of how to live a life with love at the center.

My early readers and steadfast cheerleaders: Joon Ae Haworth-Kaufka, James Tate Hill, Lydia Kiesling, Lee Bacon, Mim Turnbull, Delphine Bedient, Rachel Powers, Chris Lang, Joe Mansfield, Raechel Frogner, James Yu, and Leah Sanchez. You are the best.

Anah Tillar for the last-second course correction.

The ladies across the street.

Faith Black Ross for loving this book and fielding last-second panicked emails with calm aplomb. From the courts of Manhattan to now, it's been a wonderful ride.

Nebojsa Zoric for the stunning cover.

The whole team at Crooked Lane. You run such a tight ship and it's appreciated more than you know. Special shout out to: Rebecca Nelson, Madeline Rathle, and Dulce Botello.

And finally, always and forever, Tiffany Koyama Lane. You are my biggest supporter and the love of my life. Our house sometimes leaks, we rarely get enough sleep, and our feet hurt thanks to all the Legos we step on, but there is nobody else's name I'd rather get tattooed on my heart.